M

WHEN LOVE RETURNS

for Gabriola's volunteer firefighters
with thanks

WHEN LOVE RETURNS

BY
VANESSA GRANT

MILLS & BOON LIMITED
ETON HOUSE   18–24 PARADISE ROAD
RICHMOND   SURREY   TW9 1SR

*First published in Great Britain 1991
by Mills & Boon Limited*

© Vanessa Grant 1991

*Australian copyright 1991
Philippine copyright 1991
Large Print edition 1992*

ISBN 0 263 12978 0

*Set in Times Roman 16 on 16½ pt.
16-9203-55680 C*

*Printed and bound in Great Britain by
William Clowes, Beccles, Suffolk.*

CHAPTER ONE

THREE steps towards the summer-house, Julie realised she had forgotten to roll up the windows and lock her car. Nothing new in that, she admitted wryly. Years ago, David had once lectured her about carelessness until she cried.

The heels of her beige Italian court shoes sank into the soft ground as she turned back to her small red Suzuki. Julie tensed as the sound of hammering echoed through the trees, her fingers curling around the door-handle. What on earth was that sound? Building contractors launching an invasion on peaceful Gabriola Island?

She closed her eyes, breathing in the scent of sweet honeysuckle blossoms as she listened to the hidden pounding. A woodpecker! Of course! She strained her senses, but there were no cars, no sirens, just the incredibly noisy bird...and, further away, one of the McNaughton calves bawling for its mother.

Deliberately, she tossed her bag through the open car window on to the driver's seat. Surely even David McNaughton wouldn't get excited about locking up on Gabriola Island!

On the cabin, the shingles were littered with scraps from the drooping branches of the tall, sheltering cedar trees. The cedar siding had once been a warm brown. Now it was bleached white from time and sunlight. Julie loved everything about this place, yet she had neglected it for the last eight years. Foolish. She had thought the cottage would be haunted, but there were only summer smells...and solitude.

How often had David looked up at the empty summer home, thinking critical thoughts about its owner? She shook that thought away, knowing how insane it was for a grown woman to worry that she had failed her childhood idol's standards.

The front door creaked as she swung it inwards. Inside, there was only emptiness and dust, a musty smell over everything. Miraculously, the windows were intact. Where else but Gabriola could you abandon a house for years, come back and find it untouched? She should have come years ago, but she might well have stayed away another eight years if her brother hadn't been so persistent last weekend.

Sunday dinner was a family occasion for the Charters. Julie usually came alone. It wasn't worth subjecting a man to her mother's matchmaking urges. Between Mom's, 'Are you seeing anyone?' and Dad's words of wisdom on how to get promoted to headmistress, Wally liked to give his kid sister some Sunday advice. Julie usually escaped the barrage by playing with her nephews. Last Sunday, both of Wally's boys had been away at computer camp, leaving Julie firmly at the mercy of big-brother wisdom.

'Time to get that cottage of yours on the market,' Wally had insisted. 'A new coat of paint on the inside walls, a good cleaning. Mow the lawn and put up a For Sale sign.'

She had been oddly irritated at Wally's invasion of the summer home that had been her share of the divorce settlement. 'That's not a lawn. It's a ground cover that doesn't need tending. They call it——'

'I'll handle it for you if you like.'

Julie had hidden a smile. Wally would handle anything—for a commission.

'Now's the time, before interest rates go up again and kill the market for summer homes.'

Her mother had slid a steaming apple pie on to the table and Julie had heard herself say, 'I'm going over to the island next week.'

She had wondered uneasily how tarnished all the old fantasies of Mountainview would be after eight years. David had dubbed the hilltop Mountainview before the land was subdivided, long before Tom's parents had built the cottage as a wedding present for Tom and Julie.

Like everything else, Gabriola and Mountainview would have changed.

But they hadn't, she realised now. An island removed from time. Today she had driven past the McNaughton farm on her way up here, had seen smoke wisping from the chimney. She had not heard David's name in years, but he would be there. Once, she would have been drawn to the wisp of smoke, might have run to fling herself into his arms. But if she went down to the farm, Sandy would be smiling that mother earth smile, and David...

David had always known what he wanted from life. It had taken Julie longer, that was all. She had made mistakes, but her life was exactly as she wanted it now. She loved the challenge of teaching at Unlimited Potential. Loved her new condo in Vancouver's False

Creek. Loved evenings at the theatre, weekends exploring the waterfront.

Loved Mountainview cottage on Gabriola.

She had known it was stupid to come back, and yet—criminal to leave a beautiful cottage unoccupied just because Julie Charters Summerton couldn't bring herself to make a decision. Silly to hang on to Mountainview, unthinkable to sell it.

Perhaps she would stay here this summer. She had the new English Literature course to write. What better place, with the deer outside her door and the fresh sea air blowing across the peak of the hill?

Did the deer still wander the island? Could she look out at sunset and find warm brown Bambis grazing on the wild field grass?

She swung around impatiently, focusing on a small speck on the counter. Of course there would be mice—no cat in residence. An empty rural house. Certainly there were plenty of spiders' webs, clinging to the rafters. Nature had been nibbling away for eight years, but Julie wasn't about to start scrubbing now! Not dressed in a white skirt and sweater, clothes that had cost her two weeks' pay!

The sun warmed her face as she stepped back outside. Wonderful smells—cedar and maple. Frogs out back in the pond. A bumble bee cruising past. Did the ducks still come to nest at the edge of the pond each year? They'd used to, ever since David had dug out the hollow with his bulldozer.

Strange that David's memory was more a part of this place than Tom's. That David had always been more *real* than anyone else in her life. When Julie was ten, he had been a quiet, infallible nineteen. When she was thirteen... Her face flamed at the memory, but she supposed David had understood. Or had he forgotten?

If she really was going to stay, she had better get the ferry across to Nanaimo before the stores closed. The fact that she hadn't packed jeans and a cotton shirt seemed stupid now, but she had really intended to breeze in and look the place over, then lock the door again and——

Forget the place for another eight years?

She stopped halfway between the house and the car, her eyes trying to see around the corner of the path. Were the ducks down there on the pond? She took one step towards the path and felt her shoe sliding on the loose soil. She bent to take off her shoes.

Be practical for once in your life, Julie!

She smiled at David's echo. David, as always, was right. If she left now, she could buy jeans and trainers in Nanaimo. Cleaning supplies too. If she hurried, she could be back to see the sun set. She closed her eyes, warmed by the echo of old sunsets. She breathed in deeply and felt lighter, freer. Tom and Julie. They had been friends more than lovers. Even the marriage had not been momentous enough to leave lasting pain. Silly to stay away all these years.

She started her little car, humming as she reversed down the drive. She had never forgotten the shape of this drive. She could still speed backwards down it, her hands instinctively controlling the shiny little car. She could hear the grass in the middle of the drive rushing against the underside of her car. As her car's back wheels crested on the culvert, Julie swung the steering-wheel to turn neatly out on to Mountainview Lane.

David changed gear and urged the old dump truck over the peak of the hill. He would dump this load of gravel at Patrick's, then go back to the farm. Tomorrow morning he would move the back hoe from the gravel pit, take it over to Pat's place. David didn't do landscaping services much any more, hadn't time for it and didn't need the extra money. This time was different, though. His brother Pat wanted to surprise his new wife.

David was smiling as the burdened dump truck started to pick up speed on the gravel road. Somehow, Molly the dinosaur lady fitted right into his brother's life. David was not a fanciful man, but he could easily picture Molly and Pat bent over a small baby some time in the future. It would be nice to have more kids around the place. The farm seemed so empty now with Stanley gone to university, working summers in the city. If it weren't for Sarah's two kids stopping by, David's home would have been echoing loneliness.

He frowned as he turned on to Mountainview Lane. He should go up for a look at Julie's place. Not now, with the truck loaded, but after he had delivered the load to Pat's. He had chased some hikers off last week. He shifted into third gear and squinted against the sun, suppressing the familiar irritation. Damn Julie, couldn't she either sell, or come and look after the place? She——

A flash of red in the corner of his eye.

A car! A car shooting out from the drive!

Abruptly, he slammed the shift lever down to second. Not enough time—too close. Slow-motion horror, no time at all. His loaded truck. Twelve yards of gravel. Threshold breaking. Not too much or he'd be steering a wild thing, out of control. He pulled down another gear. The engine screamed, the brakes. If he lost control of—surely whoever it was——

Little red car, hurtling on to the road. He jerked the wheel. So small, inconsequential bit of red metal. Hit the ditch, try to ride it— somehow, miss that car. He felt nausea rising up, could see smashed red metal after the impact.

The car, backing *towards* him! A bloody tourist, driving around, looking at the trees instead of—— His front wheel bit the ditch. David heard the scream of gravel, knew with sickening certainty that he would skid, moving sideways, ripping up the ditch and skating towards that car! He stepped desperately on the throttle, trying for forward momentum to regain control, pull off the road.

The wheels caught—heavy truck, impossibly small car. No one in the car would have a chance if—— He saw the red car jerk, change direction. Inertia carried both vehicles another twenty feet along the gravel.

Then, suddenly, it was over. Quiet. The echo of violence. A cloud of dust rising all around.

David fumbled with the door, but it would not open. He slid across and out the passenger side. His feet hit the gravel. Heartbeat. Breath. Then bleeding. First-aid procedures scattered through his mind as he tore around the front of the little car. It had to have been a hell of a blow. The whole back end of the car was caved in. The driver——

He tore the driver's door open, demanded roughly, 'Are you hurt?' praying for an answer. A woman! A wild riot of warm auburn curls everywhere.

Pain seized his chest. Julie! If he had killed Julie...

Julie saw the truck in her rear-view mirror. The tuneless song on her lips died to nothing. She tried to brake, get into first gear and *moving*, away from it, but there was no time. Monstrously big, massive dump truck.

Only a total idiot went screaming out of a driveway without even *looking*! Her eyes were frozen on the rear-view mirror, watching the hulk grow larger and larger. Then, suddenly, it slewed sideways.

She had a terrifying vision of the truck pulverised against a tree, the driver dead. The gravel pit at the end of Mountainview Lane was on McNaughton land. It had to be David in the truck, coming from the pit. Why else would a truck be...? She would live the rest of her life knowing she had killed David.

She heard the scream, and it was her own voice. Then she felt the impact. The truck slammed into the side of her car, slewing sideways, taking her on a wild ride of suspended terror. They would both die, she and David. Forever...

Finally there was nothing at all but the echo of screaming metal and her own voice fading into the settling dust on the road ahead. She was still staring into the rear-view mirror when he strode around the front of her little Swift— alive. He was alive! She tried to free her fingers, could not seem to move anything.

The door jerked open so quickly that she had the illusion she would fall out. She heard the urgency in his voice, and tried to turn to look at him. The nightmare would not release

her. The truck splattered against a big old tree.
David, slumped motionless over the wheel.

'Julie?' His hand closed on her shoulder.

She managed to turn to look at his face.
Her first thought was that he had not changed
at all, but of course he was older. He was tall,
broad, his face marked by the sun and the
wind. He was wearing a battered baseball cap
as a shield against the sun. Black curls twisted
to freedom around the edges of the cap as his
eyes raked grimly over her body.

'Are you hurt?'

She swallowed. His fingers tightened on her
shoulder.

'Julie? Can you move?' She must have
nodded. He snapped, 'Get out of the car.'

She stared at her hands, fingers curling
around the steering-wheel.

'I can't haul you out of there until I know
if you're hurt.' His voice was filled with suppressed anger. 'Does it hurt at all to breathe?'

He crouched on the gravel beside her open
driver's door, his eyes dark and concerned.
She felt a shudder go through her. Any minute
she would get words together. His hand
moved, exploring her shoulders, her arms,
impersonal over her breasts as they probed for
a sign of injury to her ribs. She wondered how

his touch would feel if she were the woman he loved.

'Thank God you had your seat-belt on,' he said harshly. 'Can you move your legs?' His hand was on her thigh, probing, watching her face for signs of pain. 'You're in shock,' he decided.

She almost caught his hand back when he drew it away. He was right about the shock. It was years since she had succumbed to fantasy about David McNaughton. She supposed that he was always there, in the background of her mind, but the dreams had stopped forever the day he told her about Sandy.

Childish fantasies.

'Come on, Julie. I want you out of here.' He captured her hand, pulled gently, watching her face for any sign of pain. The steering-wheel was in his way. He was touching her so carefully. Anyone else might haul her out, but of course David would think of the possibility that shock might mask pain. David always did think first.

'Julie, swing your legs out.'

Somehow, her body obeyed.

'Now stand up.'

She swallowed, staring at the twist of dark hair that escaped the fabric of his shirt where it was open at his throat. He was so close. What had come over her? David... This was ridiculous! After all these years!

He crouched down in front of her, thigh muscles bulging in his battered old jeans. 'Dizzy?' he demanded.

She shook her head.

The lines at the corners of his eyes were deeper than they had been, but his eyes were that deep brown, still framed by heavy dark lashes. Yes, he was older. The cleft in his chin was deeper, sharper, and there were threads of silver among his black curls.

'It's different to have you so silent.' He was almost smiling, urging her with his hands. 'Come on, stand up. I know you're shaken, but I've got to get you away from this car.' He held her as she stood, his arm around her shoulder. 'OK?' he demanded, staring down at her.

'Yes.'

'So you *can* talk.'

She closed her eyes, heard the sound of an eagle somewhere. He felt hard and strong beside her, holding her. He swung her into his arms and she felt dizziness as he hurried across the road, carrying her. She had no idea where she thought he would take her, but in the end he deposited her on a big old tree stump at the edge of a clearing. She felt so strange, disorientated. His arms around her, holding her safe. Today's hard, warm David meshed with the memories.

'Stay there!' he ordered.

'Where are you going?'

He ignored her question. Silly to think she could stop him, but if those fumes ignited... Julie shuddered and closed her eyes. She heard him come back a minute later, the gravel crunching under his boots. At any moment this could turn into an unpleasant scene.

She asked, 'Is your truck damaged very badly?'

When he didn't answer, she opened her eyes. He was staring at her, that old look, somewhere between worry and anger. He was wearing old faded jeans and a sleeveless sweatshirt that left the muscles of his arms hard and prominent. He closed his eyes briefly, said harshly, 'I could have killed you, Julie. I damned near did. Bloody luck you don't have two tons of gravel truck and twelve yards of gravel taking you to your grave.'

'I always was lucky.' She tried to smile, but his eyes would not answer hers.

'Luck? More like stupidity! One day you'll kill yourself with your nonsense!' His legs were slightly astride, his stance big and dangerous—dark man; tall, muscular, angry. She felt the old breathless fear of childhood. Running up against David, holding her own, driven somehow to make him angry. His voice, growling, 'It's no bloody different than it was when you were a kid! Damn it, Julie, when are you going to grow up? Do you think I'll always be there to bail you out?'

She shivered and hugged herself tightly. 'There's never anyone on this road. I didn't stop to think that——'

'Damn it, Julie Charters! Do you *ever* think?' He glared at the trees framing the mountains on the mainland. 'I was there, wasn't I? Your driving out of that lane without looking—that's about as bright as diving into our bull pen when you were twelve.'

'Patrick dared me.' David snorted, and Julie couldn't help smiling at the way her own words sounded. Childish, and of course it had been, but she'd always been a sucker for a dare, and David's younger brother had always been a tease.

'And today? Who dared you to back into my damned dump truck?'

She shook her hair back, felt the curls springing free around her shoulders. She'd had two ornate combs holding the curls back, but they were gone now.

'Well?' demanded David.

'Is your truck damaged?' Her voice turned aggressive. Somehow he could always do this, turn her to anger and rebelliousness. She got to her feet impatiently, kept moving to cover the sudden unsteadiness. Shock, that's all it was. She certainly wasn't hurt.

'Damaged?' He shrugged. 'I haven't tried moving it yet, but the driver's door won't open.'

'Sorry,' she muttered. Damn the man! He made her feel like an irresponsible teenager again.

'You're sorry?' He hooked his thumbs in his belt. 'I need that truck, you know. Some of us have to work for a living.'

'I work for a living,' she snapped back. 'Probably harder than you!'

He laughed, but his eyes were hot and black. 'Play-work. I'm sure your divorce settlement covered most of your needs.'

'You——'

'Oh, hell, Julie!' He raked one hand through the black curls, dislodging his cap. 'I don't know what made me say that. You always——'

'Bring out the worst in you?' She tried to ignore her heart beating with hard, breathless gasps. The sun overhead, beating down summer. David's harsh anger echoing. As if there had been no time between. They'd hardly spoken during the years she was married to Tom. The last time they'd *really* talked to each other had been shouting and screaming when she was seventeen. And before that, all the way back to her thirteenth birthday.

He made an explosive sound. 'I don't usually carry on verbal wars.'

'Only with me?'

'You can be so damned exasperating.' His lips turned down, but the laughter was lurking in his eyes now.

She said defensively, 'My insurance will cover the damage to your truck.'

'That's my Julie!' He laughed. 'Let someone else look after the chaos you've caused.'

'That's not fair! Oh, lord!' She grimaced and made her voice quiet, but the anger was still there, boiling up. 'I don't run around causing chaos, and I don't leave other people to look after my messes. And what the hell do you think insurance is for, anyway? If you think I won't pay for—— Have you any idea how my insurance rates are going to sky-rocket after this?'

He growled, 'At least you have insurance.'

She said rigidly, 'It's against the law not to have auto ins——'

'Or you wouldn't? I can believe that.' The laughter was all gone. She saw his fingers curl, as if he wanted to shake sense into her.

She muttered, 'Will you shut up?'

He shrugged. 'Does it occur to you that I need that truck? That I can't afford to have it laid up weeks for repairs?'

She snarled, 'Some of us have to work for a living?' echoing his earlier words. 'You're a great one to talk, David McNaughton! You and your damned relatives owning half this island. You——'

'That's a wild exaggeration.'

She exploded, landing on her feet on the field grass with a soft thump, pacing away, then back, unsteady in her city shoes. 'That's David! Pick up on the mistakes! Let's be accurate by all means—even in the middle of a raging battle! Gentleman farmer! You'd probably float to your grave in comfort if you never dug another ditch for those cows! You——'

'Julie, shut up.'

She broke off, knowing from the look in his eyes that he would not hesitate to shake sanity into her. She could still hear the echo of her own voice from the trees, hysterical, raging, screaming at him.

A big bumble bee circled David's head, but he ignored it.

'How the hell do you do it, David?' She bit her lip. 'I'm sorry. I'm sorry I hit your bloody truck, but you've got the greatest talent for rubbing me the wrong way...'

'Yeah. Well...' He ran his hands roughly through his hair. 'Forget about the truck. You'll have enough problems over this without my adding to it by putting an insurance claim on it.'

She shook her own hair back, finger-combing it and finding it wildly tangled.

'David,' she said breathlessly, 'I'm not a kid. You don't need to protect me. Of course you'll put——'

He shook his head abruptly. 'When I saw that car—— Have you any idea how small that car of yours looks from the cab of my truck?'

She pushed damp hands down along her skirt. 'Look, could you—please stop raking me over the coals.'

'Raking you——' He caught his rising voice and said rigidly, 'Don't you ever take anything seriously? You could have been killed!'

'All right! I know it!' She could have caused David to die trying to avoid the accident. She knew that too, but could not say the words with his eyes watching her, criticising what they saw. Her fingers clenched in on themselves and she managed to calm her voice. 'Could you just stop it? I don't need a David lecture—I've had enough of them in my life. So I made a mistake. I can look after it. I'm sorry if your truck's laid up, but I can't do much about that either. I'll certainly make sure my insurance pays for—— I—— There's a car coming.'

He turned to look over his shoulder. 'Police.'

'On a sleepy place like Gabriola, with one RCMP cruiser, how on earth——?'

He jerked his head towards the dump truck. 'I called them from the truck.'

She grimaced. 'You've got a phone in your truck? Why did you call? To get me charged with careless driving?'

'Driving without due care and attention?' he said softly. 'No, of course not. But it's got to be reported. There's surely more than five hundred dollars' worth of damage done to that little bug of yours.'

She felt tired suddenly. 'And, being David, you go by the rules?'

He said drily, 'It wouldn't hurt you to go by the rules. Like looking before you cross the street. And anyway, you can't take that car in for repairs on insurance without an accident report.'

Predictably, he was right. Being right was one of David's more irritating qualities. She said wearily, 'Damn you, why don't you get out of my life? Go home to your wife.'

She knew she was being unreasonable, but somehow he did that to her. Whenever she saw criticism in his eyes, heard censure in his voice, something deep inside her snapped.

He said quietly, 'Sandy died, Julie. Three years ago.'

CHAPTER TWO

JULIE'S eyes flew to David's—deep brown,
quiet. David alone? Without Sandy, the
woman he had loved so deeply?

'I . . . David, I'm sorry.'

'I know.' He touched her shoulder, almost
as if *he* were comforting *her*. Up on the road,
a car door slammed. David said gently, 'Sorry
about the police, but it's got to be reported.'

'I know. I——' Standing in the midst of a
green clearing on Gabriola, shouting at
David. Julie sighed. Some things didn't
change . . . except that they *had* changed. She
wanted to touch him, tell him how sorry she
was about Sandy. Words weren't enough. She
wanted . . . to know why, what had happened,
but arguing with David was one thing . . . she
wouldn't want to say anything to hurt him.

She said only, 'How's Stanley?' She remembered David's son as ten years old, shy
and skinny and worried that he would be
forever small.

'Off at university.'

From the road, an official voice called out, 'Anybody hurt?'

David shouted back, 'No. We're fine! Just two of us, over here.'

He walked away from her, towards the uniformed man standing on the gravel road. Julie followed more slowly, picking her way over the uneven ground. A dry summer. August now and the grass was starting to brown, the cedar and Douglas fir dark green all around. Every time she looked up, she saw David's back moving away from her. So many years, but she would have recognised him anywhere, any time, just seeing the way he moved, that slow walk that ate up the ground. He never seemed to hurry, but she remembered trying to keep up, running behind, calling out his name. His shoulders, swinging slightly with his movement, broad and steady.

When she got to the road, the officer was muttering, 'Sure made a mess of that car, didn't it?'

Even here on Gabriola, an accident meant paperwork. Endless questions later, the officer tore off copies of the accident report and handed one to Julie, then added a green summons form. 'You understand that if you wish to plead guilty to this charge, you just have to pay the ticket before the date? The address is there at the bottom.'

'Yes. Thanks.' She met David's eyes, heard the officer explaining what she should do if she wished to plead not guilty. She wasn't surprised to end up with a traffic ticket for failing to yield the right of way. For once, she agreed with David about her own behaviour.

'Want me to call a tow truck for your car?' asked the officer.

Her eyes jerked back to David. He said firmly, 'I'll look after that.'

'Right.' The officer was closing his ticket book, preparing to leave. 'What about your truck?'

'It'll run,' David assured him. 'I can drive it away.'

'OK then, that's it. Can I give you a ride anywhere, Ms Summerton?'

'I——'

'I'll look after it,' said David. 'Julie's an old family friend.'

The RCMP officer smiled faintly at that. 'Right, then, I'll be off.'

Julie watched the patrol car drive away, and said dismally, 'An old family friend? Just came for a friendly collision, did I?'

David's eyes passed over her as he turned back to the vehicles tangled on the road. She felt what he was seeing, saw herself in his eyes. Her hair tangled in the wind, unruly, a city style gone wild in the country. It had been free and curling around her shoulders, attractive and shining when she started the day. Sandy would have tied her long blonde hair back to keep it from the wind. Sandy wouldn't have worn a white knit suit either. Wouldn't have driven smack into David's dump truck.

She felt anger stirring, but seemed powerless to stop it. There had never been any point to comparing herself to Sandy McNaughton. She...

Sandy was dead. Remembering that, Julie felt a sick guilt at her own feelings for the other woman. Irrational feelings, because who could find anything to dislike in David's wife?

The silence was full, uncomfortable, as if he could read her thoughts. She said uncomfortably, 'I thought you'd know him—the policeman. I—— Only a couple of RCMP on the island, and you're not on first-name terms with this one?' Her words sounded silly, felt trivial.

'This fellow's new.'

She laughed, heard the faint note of hysteria and silenced herself abruptly. David was walking around their vehicles, muttering something about their not being locked together.

'Your car's demolished,' he said flatly. 'You *have* got collision insurance on it?'

'Yes.' Julie hugged herself, staring at the front of her Suzuki Swift. From the front, it looked almost normal. At the back... 'I've just bought it. It gets terrific mileage.' It was a wonder she'd escaped alive. And David— she couldn't bear to think about what might have happened to David. She had seen the truck heading towards the ditch. Trying to avoid hitting her car, to save her. He could so easily have hit a tree, crushed himself between the load of gravel and one of those monstrous Douglas firs.

She said unsteadily, 'It's the first new car I've ever had.' It would have been her fault. David...so hard to imagine that anything could penetrate his strength, but she'd almost killed him today. She saw the look in his eyes, heard herself saying, 'Please don't tell me that——'

His open palm came down hard on the front fender of her car. She winced at the noise and he said coldly, 'You don't have right of way coming off private property.'

She opened her mouth to retaliate, then the anger abruptly drained away. What was she thinking of? Why did she always respond to him with anger? 'I—— Don't worry, I'll pay the ticket, of course. You won't land up in court, testifying against me.'

'Terrifying thought,' he said wryly.

She wondered what he would say in court if she pleaded not guilty. Of course she was guilty, but trust David to go calling the police without even warning her first. Doing the right thing, of course. By the book, according to the Motor Vehicle Act.

He had told the officer that he suspected Julie would have had trouble seeing the truck coming, that Mountainview Lane was curved just slightly, difficult to see from the drive. It wasn't true. It bothered her that he had lied for her, even a small lie.

She bit her lower lip. 'You said your truck would drive away. What if it won't?'

He pulled open the passenger door. 'Then I'll get the tractor up and tow it back to the farm.' It was a big step up into the truck. He leapt up easily, the muscles bunching in his thighs through the denim. 'Come on, Julie, let's go.'

'I—I just need a ride to the ferry.' She stared up at him, wondering how she would get up there, what to hold on to.

He stared back down at her, his eyes flat and dark. 'You need a decent meal and a good sleep before you start running around again.'

Running around. As if he'd pulled her out of the bull pen and told her to go home and stay inside for the rest of the day. She muttered, 'I can't leave my car here.'

'Do you think someone's going to steal it?' The laughter was in his eyes, his lips just slightly turned down at the corners. How often had she looked for laughter in his eyes? Old memories. Why on earth were they surfacing now?

'It's——I can't just leave my car in the middle of the road.' Her heart was beating heavier with each stroke—fear, excitement. She was not certain which, but knew it was a warning signal. Don't get into that truck with David.

'To quote you, "there's never anyone on this road".' He jerked his head impatiently. 'Come on.' He stretched out a hand and she felt hers folded in it. He was bigger, harder, stronger. He took her weight easily, pulling her up into the cabin of the truck. Afterwards, her hand crawled with tingles, as if he had held too tightly.

For all the truck's battered look, it was clean inside. She pulled the door closed and sat with her hands curled together, jumping when David reached for the gear lever. The dark hairs on the back of his hand brushed against her arm. She stared at his hand, so close to her arm. His skin was dark against her pale whiteness.

The engine growled as he changed gear.

She stared through the windscreen as he reversed to clear her crumpled little car. 'I was going to stay at my place tonight,' she said stiffly.

She glanced at him and was hit with an overwhelming impression of hard muscles and a grim mouth that said critically, 'You haven't been there in years.'

She opened her lips to protest, then pressed them closed. David would always disapprove of her decisions, always had. She said quietly, 'It's dusty, but the walls and windows are intact. I know it's been a long time. I've—I was going to move in and clean it up.'

'Move in?'

'For the rest of the summer.' She shifted uneasily, staring at a dark smear on the front of her white skirt. The cleaners would never be able to get it out.

'Where do you live now?'

'Vancouver. One of those condos at False Creek.'

She watched the hard thrust of his thigh muscles as he urged the truck gently through the drainage ditch beside the road. 'A False Creek condo? And free for the summer? I thought you said you worked for a living?'

'I'm a teacher. Summer vacation.' Her voice sounded defensive, even to her own ears. Why should she feel like that? Why explain to him? Even her holiday was a working vacation. She had contracted to write two new courses for Unlimited Potential's grade twelve curriculum during the summer break. She closed her lips. Years too late to try to persuade David that she was not an irresponsible fool.

He said quietly, 'One of those condominiums on a teacher's salary? I guess I don't have to worry that you got a fair settlement out of Tom, do I?'

She snapped, 'If you must know, the condo's on a sub-lease. But you don't have to

worry about me at all. Control your big
brother urges, David. I already have a
brother.'

His eyes flashed with real amusement.
'Who's going to stop you smashing into the
other side of my truck? My memory of Wally
doesn't cover it.' He changed gear again. The
truck lurched through the ditch as he ma-
noeuvred around her car. 'You can stay at the
farm tonight. You'll want cleaning supplies
and bug spray before you move into the
cottage. Wouldn't hurt to put a cat over there
for a couple of days, too, to get rid of the
mice. As I recall, you're not very fond of
being woken in the night by mice.'

Her face flushed as the back wheels
bounced at the bottom of the ditch. She had
been eleven. Patrick must have been fifteen
and Sarah around thirteen. There had been
others, four or five of them, local children
and summer kids like Julie, all enthused at
the idea of sleeping out in the McNaughtons'
hayloft. As Julie remembered the incident, the
parents had been opposed to the idea until
twenty-year-old David volunteered to sleep
out with them to watch over the bunch.

She had woken in the middle of the night,
had lain shivering under her sleeping-bag as

she listened to the persistent rustling somewhere nearby. Rustling, scurrying. Something chewing? She had tried to wipe out the sound, but when the mouse scurried near, touching her hair, she had flown trembling and crying to the sleeping David. He had woken abruptly, listening quietly to her whispered panic. She remembered how strong his arms had been. He had held her, comforted her, told her the names of the stars they could see through the open door in the hayloft. By the time he suggested that she go back to her sleeping bag, the mouse seemed a distant fantasy.

Julie stared at his hands on the steering-wheel, long-fingered, square, strong. Like his arms around her. Even after all these years, she could close her eyes and remember the feel of his arms, strong and sure and safe. She had been terrified of the teasing that would come the next day, but David had never told anyone about her cowardly reaction in the middle of the night. If he had, Patrick would surely have teased her mercilessly.

She said unevenly, 'I was going to get cleaning things. And some jeans. I know that—I could go to Sarah's, couldn't I? If your sister and her husband are still running

a bed and breakfast, I could stay there tonight. You don't need to——'

'It's August.' David slowed the truck and
turned right. Towards the farm, not towards
Sarah and Edward's. 'They're booked up to
the end of September.'

'Well, there must be somewhere on the
island. Somewhere...else.'

'Not this time of year. Not without reservations.' He geared up again, roaring along
the road beside his own pasture. Julie could
see the cows clumped around what looked like
a pond over to the left.

'I could go to Nanaimo. You could take me
to the ferry.' She felt unreasonably panicked
at the prospect of a night at David's farm.
'Or there's a taxi service, isn't there?'

'Don't be silly.'

She hadn't stayed at the farm since...
before Sandy came. She turned to stare out
of her window. It was probably true that you
should not try to go back to old places, old
memories. Back to that perpetual antagonism
between her and David, war hovering, just
waiting the opportunity to snap out and surge
over her...over them. She *did* have a hot

temper, but there couldn't be a man in the world who roused it more easily than David McNaughton.

Stubbornness—that's what it was. David's stubbornness always rubbed her the wrong way. And now, if he had decided she should stay at the farm, she would have a hell of a fight changing his mind.

She grimaced and asked, 'How are your parents?'

'Fine.'

Maybe it would be all right. She could talk to Mrs McNaughton, ask about the garden and the tomato crop. And the roses. There had always been a rose garden in the hollow below the farmhouse.

'Is your dad still working on the farm?'

'Not since his heart attack.' David slowed and turned into the gate. 'I'll settle you first, then I'll go dump this load of gravel at Pat's.'

She swept one hurried glance over the homestead—the beautiful old farmhouse, lush garden, corrals down the hill, the chicken house, a barn. She was uncertain what the other buildings were. No sign of Mr McNaughton, but there was a small pick-up truck near the house. 'I didn't know your dad had a heart attack. How——?'

'It was mild, just enough to get him to quit smoking and watch his diet. And lay off the heavy work.'

'It'll be nice to see him. And your mom.' She felt stilted.

He said, 'They're not here. They're following the circuit with the show string.'

'The what?'

'The circuit. Taking a couple of heifers and a cow-calf pair round for showing.'

'Why?'

He stopped the truck in front of the farmhouse. It was just as she remembered, a sprawling west-coast-style home with a big, covered veranda. David turned and stretched his arm along the back of the seat behind her. She could feel the warmth from his body. His lips were turned slightly down, amusement in his eyes.

'We raise Limousin cattle to sell as breeding stock. Didn't you know that?'

'Sort of. I just never—— You take the cows to shows? To sell them?'

'More or less—PR stuff, to get the strain we breed better known. If nobody knows we've got good breeding stock, we won't sell many bulls, won't get cows brought here to service.'

'To service?' She flushed, suddenly understanding. 'I—so they—do you take the cows
to shows every year?'

'Yes, we do. At least, *I* don't do it if I can
avoid it. I'd rather be here than on the circuit.
Dad likes it, though. Are you going to get
out?'

'Am I—what?'

'I can't get out of the truck until you do.'
His lips curved up slightly. 'My door's
jammed.'

She pushed open the heavy door and
scrambled down. Why did she feel so self-
conscious? The antagonism between them was
normal, but this uncomfortable feeling of
awareness...

'I——David, I need my suitcase.'

'Where is it?'

She turned and found herself staring up at
his eyes, golden flickers of light in their deep
brown. Her hair blew across her face, and she
pushed her hands through it, holding it
against the light wind. 'In my boot.'

'Forget it, then.' His eyes tangled in her
hair, dropped to the fabric of her sweater
where it was pulled tight by her uplifted arms.
She flushed and dropped her arms, but his
voice was neutral, empty of emotion. 'You'd

need a cutting torch to get that boot open.
You'll have to wait for the insurance appraisal before you can get the case out.'

Her poor car. 'Do you think they'll be able
to fix it?'

'Anybody's guess.' He shrugged. 'They
might write it off and pay you out. You
probably won't know for a couple of days
after it gets to the appraisal centre.'

'You seem quite knowledgeable about the
process.' Her lips twitched. 'Do you get in a
lot of accidents, David? Tourists running into
your truck?'

'Stanley wiped out my car on the Island
Highway last summer. I got some practice.'

She wished her heart would stop beating
like that—erratic, wild. Just because he was
smiling down at her as if... 'Stanley—university, you said? He'll be on summer vacation, won't he? What's he taking?'

'Agriculture, but he's playing with a band
this summer.' David's lips twitched. 'It's a
toss-up whether he'll turn into a farmer or an
itinerant musician.'

She followed him up the stairs to the farmhouse. He bent to unlace his boots in the mud-
room. He was hard and muscular, no softness
anywhere, but if his son decided to be a mu-

sician he would accept it. She looked away, staring through the doorway into the kitchen.

'In Nanaimo?' she asked. 'He's working in Nanaimo?'

He put his boots neatly against the wall and gestured for her to precede him into the kitchen. He strode over to the sink and began filling the reservoir of an electric coffee maker.

She looked around, trying to match this kitchen to her memories. New cupboards, she decided. Warm varnished oak in place of the old painted yellow. 'What happened to the old percolator? There always used to be a coffee-pot on the wood stove. Your mom—— What happened to the stove?'

'Progress.' He slid the reservoir into its holder. 'No one but Mom could make decent coffee in that thing. As for the stove... electric's more convenient.'

'You're destroying my illusions.' She smiled and his eyes answered her. 'There I sit in the city, thinking you're pure and natural out here, and all the while you're contaminated with modern conveniences!'

She watched him scoop coffee grounds into the filter. With his parents on the show circuit and Stanley at university, he must be living alone here. Making his own meals, coming home to an empty house after a hard day's work. She bit her lip and concentrated on his words.

'... go on burning wood forever. It takes a long time to grow a tree. We'll run out of them. Besides, Sandy always hated that old wood stove.'

He said his wife's name naturally, as if she were still alive. Julie stared at his back as he turned the coffee-maker on. Was three years long enough to erase pain? To blur her image on his heart?

She remembered David's voice, years ago, telling her about Sandy... The perfect woman for me. Quiet and womanly and loving. Crazy that the memory was so sharp and clear. She bit her lip and asked hurriedly, 'Where is Stanley's band? What's he doing in it? Singing? Playing something?'

'Both.' David was watching her, frowning now. 'My son seems to be a musical virtuoso. Lord knows where he gets it from—although one of Sandy's cousins is pretty handy with a guitar.'

'Is the band in Nanaimo? Will Stanley be home tonight?'

'Victoria. I haven't seen much of him this summer.' He saw the unease in her eyes and said, 'Come on, Julie, you're surely not afraid I'll attack you in the night? You'll be quite safe with me.'

Of course she was safe with him. The heat flooded her face. This must be some insanity that hit when a woman turned thirty. Looking at David and feeling as if—— She rubbed her hands down along her skirt. 'I'll call the wreckers myself, shall I?' Her voice was brittle. 'I hate the word *wrecker*. I hope it's not a wreck. It's such a—— What will you do about your truck? About fixing the door? I'll pay for it if the insurance won't, David. I——'

'Cut it out, Julie.' He moved impatiently. 'You can have Sarah's old room for the night—you know where it is. Go up and see what you can find there while I call for the tow truck. There might be a pair of old jeans in the dresser. You'll want to change, won't you?'

'Yes,' she agreed. Trust David to remind her that she was a mess!

Sarah's room had changed. Of course, Julie had not been in this bedroom since her teens. The last time...Sarah had been getting ready to go to college, her room in chaos and clothes everywhere. David and Sandy must have been away somewhere, or Julie would not have been there. She had avoided the farm from the day David had told her about Sandy. Even back then, she had known how irrational it was. David, the first massive crush of her teenaged life.

That summer Sarah was getting ready for college...it must have been the year before Julie met Tom. She had been dreaming of going back to high school in Vancouver, meeting a boy who would love her. Sarah had been talking about leaving home, going to college, getting a degree and never marrying until she was fifty. But Julie had wanted marriage and children, and soon. Young impatience, not knowing that love did not come from running after dreams.

And the room...the curtains had been changed since then. Once there had been lambs and trees on white broadcloth. Now the drapery was muted, light browns and reds against a warm beige. Earth tones, echoed in the thick carpet. Sandy must have decorated. Earth tones would be right for the woman who was David's perfect match.

Sandy had not been able to change the view out of the window. That beautiful old dogwood tree down the hill—Julie remembered climbing its massive branches when she was eight or nine, David shouting at her to get down before she killed herself. Laughing down at David, telling him that when she grew up she would build a house for herself right under the white blossoms. David shouting back that if she wanted to grow up she'd better get out of the tree before she fell out.

Julie moved to the dresser and slid open a drawer. Leftovers from an assortment of guests over the years—a pair of brief shorts, a bikini, a fluffy beach towel. A green sweatshirt with KEEP CANADA GREEN! emblazoned on it. A pair of scarred jeans that must have been washed a hundred times.

The jeans were probably Sarah's. They were too long in the leg for Julie, a bit tight across the hips. She discarded her finely knit sweater and the light silk blouse she'd worn underneath, then pulled the big sweatshirt on and studied herself in the mirror of Sarah's childhood dresser. The green made her hair look even more fiery than usual. She had started the day feeling smart and efficient in her white suit and Italian shoes, but dressed like this she looked young and vulnerable. Luckily, the sweatshirt was big enough to conceal the way the jeans hugged her hips. She felt more comfortable with her female curves swallowed by the baggy shirt. David, all alone. She wouldn't want him to think she was trying to...

It was his fault, putting that idea in her mind. He was the one who had made that comment about not attacking her. She would never have thought of it, knew that he would never want her. And she—well, she was certainly not crazy enough to go scrambling after old childhood dreams. She wished him luck, but he would not need it. He had always been good at getting what he wanted. If she came back in a few years, she would find the farm glowing with love and warmth and... Well, that was what he should have. Another Sandy.

She pulled a small brush out of her bag and attacked the wild confusion of her naturally curling coppery curls.

'Julie?' David's voice called up the stairs. 'Do you want to come along to Pat's? Or would you rather rest here?'

She put the brush down and hurried out on to the landing, as if afraid he would take off without her. He was halfway up the stairs.

Standing there, looking down on him, she was abruptly aware of her stockinged feet. 'I'd like to come, but if it's rough going, my shoes aren't too good. I . . .'

Her voice faded. She tried to pull her eyes away from him. He must have found his way into more of her dreams than she had realised. It was insane, like a crush on a movie star, but somehow David was there in her heart. Her fantasy man, although she had never before let herself realise it.

He was staring at her. She moved her hands uneasily down the front of her denim-clad legs. His eyes seemed to be glued to her hands. When she spread them in confusion, his gaze moved slowly up over the tight denim to the sloppy sweatshirt. She hugged herself, afraid that the unwelcome physical reactions she was feeling might actually be visible. The sweatshirt was big and loose. Surely that swelling feeling in her breasts wouldn't be visible?

'I—— David—— My shoes are a bit...impractical.' She shifted, trying to break the spell. Down one step, two. He didn't move. Suddenly she was too close to him. 'Is this shirt OK? I think the jeans are Sarah's. They're a bit tight. She was always skinnier than——'

His eyes seemed to settle on the curves of her breasts and she stammered, 'I didn't — I don't know who the shirt belongs to.' She tried to get breath into her lungs quietly, but she felt strange, unsettled, breathless. 'Is it OK for me to wear it?'

'Yeah.' He cleared his throat. 'You look——' Abruptly, he stepped back, down one step. 'No need for you to come along. I'm just dumping this load of gravel, then I'll get us something for dinner.'

'Oh.' Of course he didn't really want her along with him. 'Why don't I look through the cupboards and start dinner?'

'I'll do it when I get back.' He turned and walked the rest of the way down the stairs. Halfway through the door, he tossed back, 'Check in the mud-room at the back of the house. There's a collection of shoes there. Anything that fits you, help yourself.'

She nodded, but he was already outside, heading for the truck. She hesitated, then ran down the stairs after him. He was halfway into the truck by the time she got to the front door.

'David?'

He stopped and turned, his dark eyebrows raised in a question. She licked her lower lip, too aware of his masculine body balanced on the running board of the truck. Thick, strong thigh muscles. Firm buttocks in tight denim jeans. That old sweatshirt, clinging softly to his muscles as he turned towards her.

'Do you—mind if I come? I'm not much for standing around doing nothing.' She shifted uneasily on the veranda. 'And if you don't want me to start supper—well, I could at least say hello to Pat, couldn't I? And I promise not to cause any accidents.'

He laughed then. It was so many years since she had heard his laughter that she had forgotten the warm, strong sound of it. 'Come on then, kiddo. But don't promise what you can't deliver. And find a pair of trainers in that mud-room. I'll wait.'

Kiddo? The man never had taken her seriously. Just as well, she supposed. After all, what man could be expected to listen seriously to a proposal of marriage from a thirteen-year-old girl? And of course she hadn't meant it either, not once she got older and realised how right he was, how crazily opposite and impossible David McNaughton and Julie Charters were.

She found a pair of clean but ancient trainers that were just slightly too big. They were comfortable, old enough to stand up to any abuse she might give them if she got involved in whatever David planned to do with a load of gravel at Pat's place. She tied the laces quickly and ran out to the truck, climbing up easily now that she was dressed for trucks instead of city streets.

'Haven't changed, have you?' David said in amusement as he started the truck. 'You never could stand to be left out of anything.'

She hugged herself, feeling a crazy nostalgia at sitting beside David, tagging along. 'Did you mind much?'

'No. You were good company.' He shifted and turned up McNaughton Road.

'Really?'

He shrugged, a gesture that almost persuaded her he meant it. Trust David not to be willing to say a compliment twice. Good company. He must mean it. David had never been one to make up pleasantries. He had always been the tell-the-truth-and-be-damned type.

'How's Pat?' she asked as he turned up his younger brother's drive.

'Married.'

Julie hadn't expected that, could hardly believe it. 'Who? When?'

'Molly. She illustrates children's books about dinosaurs. Sarah's kids figure they've fallen into heaven, with a dinosaur lady for an aunt.'

'She sounds...different.'

'Hm. Nice too.'

'They're happy?'

He nodded. 'Glowingly.'

She smiled, remembering Pat with his string of pretty girls. Pat, who'd always had a date, but never took any of the girls home afterwards. The man with the smooth easygoing surface and the steel underneath. 'I have trouble believing anyone got to him, but I'm glad. He deserves someone nice.'

'So does Molly, I'd say. They're still away on their honeymoon, somewhere in France, I think. This gravel is Pat's project. He wants to surprise Molly with a new jacuzzi pool when they get back.'

The hole in the ground behind Pat's house looked more like an ugly scar than a promising site for a hot pool. Julie scrambled out of the truck, asking ominously, 'How long will they be gone?'

'Another two weeks.'

'This will never be in shape in two weeks.' She wondered how easygoing Molly was.

David circled the excavation, his eyes narrowed critically. 'It always looks bad at this stage. The bedrock is close to the surface up on this hill. I had to bring in twenty loads of fill. Tomorrow I'll bring the back hoe over and get it ready for the pool. The spa man's coming on Friday. We'll have it all together in a week. Grass planted too.'

'You'll never make it. When they get back, it'll be a nightmare here.'

'Bet?' His eyes challenged hers.

'Bet,' she agreed, grinning. She would lose. If David said it would be done by Friday, of course it would, but it was fun to challenge him.

'OK,' his lips twitched, 'you're on. Now hop out of the way. I don't want to dump a load of gravel on you in my haste to win this bet.'

'You already tried to bury me under that gravel once today.' But she moved away, towards a big cedar tree that would shelter her from the gravel dumping.

'Julie——?'

She swung to face him, startled to find him close behind her. The look on his face. She swallowed, then whispered, 'I know it was my fault—really. I just...David, I...'

His hand moved slowly towards her face. She held her breath. Something inside her screamed at him. Don't touch. Stay back.

She was frozen, waiting until he slowly brushed one copper curl back, ignoring dozens of others. She felt his fingers against her cheek—rough calluses, gentle. He bent and caressed her cheek softly with his lips, and she gasped at the delicate warmth of his touch.

'What?' she breathed. 'Why?'

'I'm sorry I was so hard on you earlier, Julie.'

She was intensely aware that his eyes were on her parted lips, the tip of her tongue moistening the abrupt dryness. 'That's...all right. I—— It was my fault.'

'Yes,' he agreed softly, 'it was.' His fingers caught her chin and tilted her face up while he studied her closely. He said quietly, forcefully, 'You scared the hell out of me. I thought...do you have any idea how heavy that truck is when it's loaded? How lethal?'

He moved, and she thought her heart would never start again. His lips covered hers and it ceased to matter that she could not breathe. Seconds, a moment—endless. When his lips slowly left hers and he lifted his head, her eyes were wide and disturbed.

'Why did you do that?' she whispered.

'I've no idea,' he answered, then he turned away.

She prowled around the outside of Pat's house, wandered through the trees and finally settled on a park bench that hadn't been there a few years before. She closed her eyes and listened to the sound of David's dump truck, concentrated on planning tomorrow and the rest of her days.

Anything but remembering that kiss. It meant nothing. Just a touch, telling her how disturbed he'd been. He couldn't shake her the way he might have when she was a child. So he had kissed her instead.

Tomorrow she would go into town. She supposed she would have to go to the ICBC Claim Centre and talk to someone about her car, see if her insurance entitled her to a rental car. Then—— She had three weeks until school started again. She could—— If she had any sense, she would go back home and forget this place.

She felt a warm presence beside her. 'Hi, kitty,' she whispered. The cat was black and white, furry and purring loudly. Julie stroked absently and the cat stretched its claws gently against her denim-covered thigh.

'Whose cat are you?' she murmured. The animal merely purred in response. Julie's fingers found the soft spot on the side of the kitten's chin that all cats seemed to like. She was rewarded with increased volume on the purr. 'You like that, do you?'

Behind her, David's voice said wryly, 'It figures.'

'What does that mean?' She twisted to see him. He was watching her with an odd expression in his eyes. Confused, she bent over the cat and asked, 'Do you know her name, David?'

He pulled his hat off and sank down on the soft moss in front of the bench. 'Her? How did you know she was female?'

'Instinct, telepathy.' Julie grinned. 'A good guess. What's her name?'

'Trouble. And she's a miserable, anti-social beast.'

Julie stroked the glossy fur. 'She's a darling.'

'Oh?' He pulled a long strand of grass out of the ground. 'Your darling tore up Pat's screen window, haunted the neighbourhood with yowling, got stuck in Pat's chimney one night, wouldn't come near anyone...until Molly came.'

'The dinosaur lady?'

'Hm.' David was quietly amused. 'Sorceress, more likely. She charmed Trouble and my brother. Trouble is *almost* civilised now. Sarah's kids can feed her, but only Molly can pet her.'

Julie's brows lifted. The kitten settled more firmly into her lap.

'And you,' added David. 'Which figures, I suppose.'

'Why does it figure?' She had heard the frown in his voice, and frowned back at him. 'Is that a compliment?'

'I'm not sure.'

Trust David to be honest rather than flattering. Julie bent over the cat, enjoying the glossy sleekness under her fingers, the rewarding purr. 'It's strange, being here, looking at that house. I remember when Pat was building it.'

David leaned back against a tree trunk, his legs stretched out lazily in front of him. He had the look of a strong man who had been working hard. She wondered what his callused hands would feel like if they touched other places, not just her cheek... No! She must not let herself think like that. Dreams were all very fine, but they should be at least *possible*. Either that, or so remote that a woman couldn't take them seriously.

David chewed on the end of a long strand of grass. 'That was quite a summer for you, the year Pat started the house.'

'Yes.' The cat stretched its head back and Julie rubbed gently along the exposed throat. She had been seventeen that year, restless and dissatisfied and just graduated from high school. As always, her parents had come to Gabriola for the summer. It had started as a long summer for Julie. Sarah had been gone from the farm, working the summer in Victoria. David's parents had also been away somewhere, perhaps on the show circuit, although Julie had no memory of knowing. At the farm there had been David and Sandy, with Stanley perhaps four years old.

'What kind of a year was it for you?' she asked softly. 'I remember seeing you riding the tractor, Stanley sitting up in front of you.'

David smiled at the memory. 'He's a bit big for that now.'

'He always looked as if he enjoyed it.'

'He did. And the chickens, although it was a good thing we weren't in the poultry business, just raising eggs for ourselves.'

'He broke a lot?'

'Yeah, quite a few.'

Silence crept over them. Julie stroked the cat absently, although she could feel the restlessness in the small animal. Soon it would twist and escape her touch. Across from her, David's fingers were bending a long strand of field grass. The silence seemed complete, forever, and when she realised there were sounds, they belonged—the drone of a bee somewhere, an eagle crying overhead.

The cat stirred and she felt its fur rising. 'It's an eagle,' she said softly. 'Too big for you, Trouble.'

She saw the smile in David's eyes and said softly, 'I remember that summer, watching you. You and Sandy and Stanley.'

'I watched you too.' He snapped another piece of grass off in his fingers. 'You and Tom Summerton. I tried to tell you he was no good for you.'

'Forcefully,' she said, remembering that scene with a smile. She twisted the cat's tail gently around her hand. 'Maybe you're good at that, deciding who's good with who. Because you and Sandy...she was perfect for you.'

He said obscurely, 'That was always your problem. You thought everything was black and white.'

She shook her head. 'No, I—I remember wanting that for myself. What you and Sandy had.' She laughed self-consciously. 'Wanting it quite desperately.'

He threw the grass away, demanding harshly, 'What the hell was Tom thinking of? You were seventeen, for God's sake! He was twenty-two. He had no right——'

'I told him I was nineteen. And...' She shrugged. 'It wasn't really Tom's fault.' Tom had been Patrick's friend, come to help Pat build his house on weekends. Not a strong man, but blown with the winds. Her desire to fall in love had carried them both into an impulsive runaway marriage.

She said quietly, 'Tom didn't have a chance.'

CHAPTER THREE

JULIE gasped as Trouble's claws dug into her leg. David was halfway to his feet, as if he could somehow save her from the cat's sudden, painful launch into motion.

He said, 'I warned you, that cat's a menace. Are you hurt?'

'Nothing that won't fade quickly. She didn't mean to hurt me.' She met his eyes and said firmly, 'Any more than Tom did. He fell in love with someone else. He didn't mean to; it just happened.'

'He let it happen.' She could see the anger hidden in his eyes. 'He did the same thing when you were seventeen. Let himself be seduced by a child—you were hardly more than a child.'

She reached a hand towards him and said softly, 'It doesn't matter, David.'

'Of course it matters.' He was watching her. Those eyes never missed anything. 'You haven't married again?'

She twisted a curl around her finger. 'I like my life the way it is now.'

'You should marry again.'

'More advice?' she taunted gently.

'Not much use, is it? You never did take my advice.'

'That didn't stop your giving it.' Her laughter joined his softly, then faded. 'Next time, I'll give you approval on the prospective groom.'

David's lips twitched. 'I'm sure he'll appreciate that.'

'If he wants me——' She shrugged.

'Did you ever try waiting for what you want?' He dropped one hand to the ground, shifted and was on his feet, frowning down at her.

'So I made a mistake.' She made a face at him. 'They weren't bad years. Tom and I were good friends, and I learned something from it all.' She assessed the golden glints in his brown eyes—disturbing.

'What about children? I'd have thought you'd want children.'

The sun was slowly sinking in the western sky, the warmth of the summer day fading. She hugged herself, said defensively, 'What about you, David? I always pictured you with three or four children, sitting by the fire with kids climbing all over you. Why didn't Stanley have brothers and sisters?'

'Not all dreams come true,' he said quietly. She could feel something behind the masked eyes, and wished she had not asked that question. He moved impatiently towards the truck. 'Coming?'

'I... Yes.' She followed him slowly. She had been thirteen when David told her about Sandy. Easter holidays. That summer, she had come to Gabriola and—— She focused on his broad shoulders ahead of her, swinging slightly as he walked. She said slowly on a note of discovery, 'Sandy was pregnant when you got married?' Her words fell on the quiet of the setting sun.

David turned to meet her eyes. His were flat, without warmth or feeling. 'Is that your business?'

She shook her head silently.

His shoulders relaxed. 'It didn't make any difference.'

Of course it hadn't. A strange silence. She licked her lips, but no words came. She touched his hand, and his fingers linked with hers.

'Let's go home,' he said quietly.

Now she knew the real reason why she had stayed away from Gabriola all these years. Nothing to do with Tom's memories. It was David McNaughton. She had always yearned for David, a longing hidden from even herself. Impossible dream. Even now, with Sandy only a memory in his eyes, it was the last thing that could ever happen. She curled her fingers in on themselves when he released her hand, trapping the memory of his touch. Then she followed him to the cab of the empty truck, knowing that for once she had to be practical.

Tomorrow she would go back to Vancouver, bury herself in the work she had to finish before school started. The next time Gary suggested dinner and the theatre together, she would say yes. It was time she started seeing someone. She had tried dating after the divorce, but it seemed more trouble than it was worth. So she had drifted into a single existence, meeting girlfriends for the theatre, going to the kind of parties where conversation was as important as dancing.

That had to change now. If she reacted so strongly to David's work-hardened body, it was time she did something about her social life. Insanity to bury her woman's needs forever in an impossible childhood dream.

Not Gary, she decided. She could not face an entire evening with her upstairs neighbour. Proximity could not eradicate boredom. The trouble was, all the men she knew were men who talked about ideas, not men like David who built things and used their bodies in productive work. She had not known she could be turned on by the thought of a man's strength and hardness, although she had always felt impatient with Tom's endless talk—planning and never doing. Most of the men she knew were talkers, not men of action. If she asked, most of them would tell her what they thought she wanted to hear, not what was true.

David...

All right, so she would try to meet a different kind of man, more direct, more... physical. She would work at finding love the same way David would set upon a course of action: methodically.

Julie's project for this year. Find an attractive, muscular man with eyes like David's. Fall in love. It sounded insane, the sort of thing even David would not plan out ahead. She felt his eyes on her.

'How long are you staying, Julie?'

'I——' Only hours ago she had planned to stay for the rest of the summer. Just now, she had decided to leave in the morning. She closed her eyes, knowing it was impossible to stay, and said, 'I might go back to Vancouver tomorrow, or I might stay a while.'

'I suppose when you do decide, it'll be on impulse?'

'Probably,' she agreed. She felt an uncomfortable twist of nausea. They were so far apart, could not even see each other's views of life. So why did his opinion matter so much to her? She met his eyes and said firmly, 'When I make decisions, I go with what feels right.'

'That's an insane way to run a life. No wonder you're always in messes.'

'I'm not often in messes.' She sounded like a sulky child. How could his criticism so easily throw her when she was thirty-one years old, independent and successful and—presumably—grown up?

Grown up enough to survive all night at the farmhouse, alone with David? She would not be at risk from him in a physical sense, but . . .

* * *

He refused her offer to cook dinner, shrugged and said, 'Easier for me. I know where everything is.'

'I could help.' She watched him moving towards the cupboards with frustration. Self-sufficient—he always had been. She said, 'At least let me peel potatoes or something.'

'Do you peel many potatoes?' he asked with amusement.

'I know how.' She spread her hands, admitting, 'I buy frozen mostly. You're an expert, I suppose?'

'No more than I can help.' He grinned. 'I usually do them with the skins on—saves a lot of labour. Just relax, Julie. I'll look after dinner.'

She prowled around the kitchen, watching him take two steaks from the freezer. He slid them into the microwave and dialled a defrost cycle.

'Your beef?' she asked.

'Hm.'

'Do you sell beef right off the farm?'

'No.' He selected a handful of fresh vegetables from the crisper—lettuce, tomato, onion. 'We're seed-stock breeders—registered stock. I'll slaughter one or two in a season. Beef for the family, usually poor stock for breeding.'

'Oh.' The microwave bell rang, and he dropped the steaks into a hot pan. He was good at this—practised, quick, as if he cooked for himself all the time. She watched the steam rising from the sizzling steak. It smelt wonderful. 'What was wrong with this one?'

'Wrong?' He pulled a vicious-looking knife from a wooden block and started chopping an onion.

'You said they were poor breeding stock,' she persisted. He must think her a fool. All those summers hanging around, but she knew less than nothing about what he really did here on the farm.

He half smiled. 'Yeah. Well, I wasn't sorry to lose this yearling. He caught me in the corral one day.'

'Caught?' Her heart stopped. 'You mean...attacked?'

He nodded, and swept the finely chopped onions into the salad bowl.

She tried to tell herself that the nausea was delayed shock from the accident. 'A yearling is...a year-old calf? How big?'

'About fourteen hundred pounds. I didn't actually weigh him.'

She squeezed her eyes tightly closed. David, alone with a wild beast that weighed more than half a ton. She said faintly, 'I'm glad you got rid of him.'

He laughed. 'I didn't slaughter him for going after me, Julie. Not that alone. I was working in the corral. It happens. But this guy wouldn't have been a good breeder. Do you want a drink? Wine? Beer? I've got some apple juice too.'

'Juice, please.' The way she was feeling, the last thing she needed was alcohol.

He poured her a cool glassful, and she sipped it slowly, leaning against the counter, watching him work. 'How could you tell he wasn't a good breeder if he was only a calf?'

He quartered a tomato with the big knife. 'He didn't have very good measurements.'

'Measurements? But didn't you say he weighed——?'

He was amused. 'Not that kind of measurement.'

'What kind?'

'This is a breeding operation,' he said gently. 'We sell young bulls as breeders, or when we sell a bull, we want to be reasonably sure he's got the——' He shrugged, and she had the feeling he was laughing gently at her.

'Got the what?'

'The—er—equipment and stamina to fulfil his new owner's expectations. So we take measurements.'

She choked on a mouthful of the juice, spluttered, 'You mean you—measurements of——'

'Take a look in a breed magazine one day,' he suggested. 'When they take pictures of a prize bull, they don't emphasise his horns.'

She hadn't thought herself naïve, but she could feel her face flaming. David took mercy on her and changed the subject. 'What have you been doing since I saw you last? Aside from moving to Vancouver?'

She shrugged, walking aimlessly around the kitchen with a tall glass of juice in her hand. 'This and that. Finishing university. Teaching.' She set the glass down on an island in the middle of the kitchen. She smoothed her hands along the well-used butcher block top.

'Finishing?' David glanced at her, watching the pensive expression in her hazel eyes, the restless way she shifted her hips even while standing still. He liked watching her; he wanted to keep her talking. He asked, 'When did you start?'

'In Nanaimo, university transfer from Malaspina College, while I was married to Tom.'

Julie spoke of Tom as an old friend instead of a painful memory. David supposed it was better that way, but Tom Summerton deserved a lot of anger for what he'd done to Julie.

She turned the glass in her hand, her dark lashes fanned over her cheeks. 'I had just two years to finish after the divorce.' Another woman might have dodged the issue, replaced 'after the divorce' with 'after I moved'. Not Julie. She had always been frighteningly direct, even as a child.

She had grown up years ago, but he could remember her as a young girl, her body curved towards womanhood, her eyes trusting and innocent. He asked huskily, 'Where did you go? UBC?'

'Simon Fraser. I liked their programme better. But I took my Masters at UBC. Can't I help with something?'

He glanced at the steaks sizzling in the pan. 'Everything's fine. Are you always so restless?'

She had gained weight since he had seen her last. It suited her, woman's curves just this side of voluptuous. David clenched his jaw and concentrated on the lettuce he was tearing up for the salad. She had always been an arresting woman, full of life, her abundant red hair and those warm hazel eyes hinting at a well of sensuality. He had always sensed that sensuality in her, but today was the first time the knowledge had turned in him like a craving.

'I can't just sit here watching you cook.'

'Why not?' Would she be restless in a man's arms? Her flesh white and soft, full roundness of her breasts. He turned the steak too soon, trying to suppress the images in his mind. Would she draw in a shaken breath when he touched the naked softness of her woman's breast? When he . . .

He had to stop this! Right now! He was a man who did things deliberately, who took a woman in his arms when the time was right. Yet all day he had been fighting the need to pull her against him, to bend down and take her full mouth as deeply as a man *could* possess a woman without——

'Why don't you finish making this salad?' he suggested in a strangled voice. 'I think it needs more tomato.'

Julie moved in front of him. Her hips swung seductively as she reached for the tomato. He squeezed his eyes shut. This was Julie, for God's sake! Younger than his kid sister. He couldn't——

He turned and his eyes caught her body in profile. She had been rounding to a woman's shape even as a young thirteen, the signs clear while she was still a child. Now the woman was enough to take a man's breath away. Or drive him to madness.

He had been a man while she was still a child. But now...

Insanity, that was what it was. Madness. He should have taken her to Sarah. To hell with Sarah's load of bed and breakfast tourists. They could have made room over there. Or put her up in Pat's place. Pat and Molly would not have minded.

He had to be out of his mind! Bringing her here! What about later? The dark hours, endless, sleeping down the corridor, no more than twenty feet between their beds. He would lie awake, wondering what she wore to bed, wondering if she slept nude. He dropped the spatula.

'What did you say, David?' Julie was watching him with worried eyes, her lips parted. Warm, full lips. If he kissed them——What *had* he said? What did she *think* he had said?

'How do you want it?' he demanded. His mind served up a sensuous image that had nothing to do with steak. 'Rare,' he added grimly, 'or well done?'

He saw the hint of laughter in her warm eyes. 'Isn't medium one of my choices?'

'Medium doesn't fit you.' She had always been impulsive, a little wild. Julie. She might sleep nude. There had always been that tinge of rebelliousness in her. Naked, her soft white flesh sliding along silken sheets...

'What do you wear——?' He clenched his jaw. A man could not ask the girl next door questions like that. 'How do you want it?' he demanded. 'The steak, I mean.'

'Well done. Are you all right, David?'

He managed to nod. If he turned to face her before his imagination subsided, she would have no doubt of what was in his mind. This was *Julie*. He couldn't...*could not* do any of the wild things racing through his consciousness. Fantasies.

'David? Are you all right?'

'Fine.' He turned the second steak. 'Tired, that's all. I was up with the dawn...sick cow.' Why had he said that? It wasn't true. He gritted his teeth and suppressed a vision of Julie clad in a lazy white scrap of luxury. A teddy. Did she own one? If not, perhaps he would buy her one and... Damn!

'Did you burn yourself? David——?'

'Any minute now,' he muttered. 'Is that salad ready yet?'

David's mood seemed to improve when they began eating. Julie had not known that he grew irritable when he was hungry, but she would watch for it in future. Then...

In future? Was she losing her marbles entirely? She attacked her steak with knife and fork, keeping her eyes down. All those years when he was married to Sandy, she hadn't thought this kind of thing, not once. She had seen David often, summers here on the island, both with her parents and later with Tom. But never——

She had only once been alone with David after he had married Sandy. He had been taken up with farming, with his family. She had been growing up. The only time she remembered standing close to him, staring at his dark eyes, was the day he tried to talk her out of Tom Summerton.

'What are you thinking about?' he asked abruptly.

'The last real conversation I had with you.' She met his eyes, half smiling. 'You tried to talk me out of being involved with Tom.'

He grimaced. 'I blew that, didn't I?'

Her eyes flashed with the memory. 'You told me if I ran off with him you'd tan my hide.'

'Red flag to a bull.' He scowled. 'If I'd been a bit more perceptive, I'd have known—I should have talked to him, not you. I might have made more of an impression.'

If David had warned Tom off her, she suspected her ex-husband would have been terrified. She would have been incredibly furious with David if he had done that. She said quietly, 'I talked him into running away, you know. It wasn't his doing.'

'I could have guessed that.' His eyes stirred with something dark and confusing. 'You always were too damned persuasive.'

'I never persuaded you. Not once.' This was *not* the way to get through the evening. She toyed with her salad. 'Tell me about your sister—Sarah.'

'The bed and breakfast is a great success. Sarah and Edward are booked all the way to October the first.' He put his knife down. 'And they've got a new addition to the family. Twin babies.'

It was years since she had let herself feel yearning over other people's children. She put her fork down. 'I didn't know. Sarah and I used to write, but . . .'

'Eight years is a long time,' he finished quietly.

'I'll go see them tomorrow.' She picked up the fork again and stabbed a piece of tomato. 'But first I'd better call the claim centre and find out about my car.'

When they had finished eating, he let her clear the table and do the dishes while he went outside to do chores. He came back with a carton of fresh eggs.

'I'll use those for an omelette tomorrow morning,' she offered, ridiculously pleased when he agreed.

'Some music?' he suggested, moving into the family room.

She followed slowly, curling up at the end of a big sofa. Pictures—they were collecting in her mind, and she knew she would not be free of them for a long time. Back home, she would put on music on her stereo, close her eyes and feel David close beside her, only a hand's reach away.

They listened to Gary Fjellgaard's island songs, to Rita MacNeil singing about Nova Scotia. 'At least we agree about music,' she murmured when Robin Conners's voice flowed over them, singing his latest love song about a fisherman on the Misty Isles. 'I went to a concert he gave in Vancouver.' She opened her eyes lazily. She would keep this picture in a special place in her memories. David's long legs stretched out lazily on the carpet, his body nestled in the corner of the sofa, his arm stretched out along the back, hand half curled towards her. If she reached, she could touch his hand so easily, brush her fingers along the back of his wrist, follow the swirl of dark hairs along his forearm. Would his lips turn down in that suppressed smile if she did that? His eyes carry lights of fire for her?

What had he done in the hours before she smashed into his truck? What time did his day start? Was it true that farmers got up with the sun? When she got up for school at six-thirty, was he already dressed and outside working? Doing what?

This was a different David from the one in her memories, comfortable and relaxed rather than hard at work, dressed in clean jeans and a loose fisherman's sweater. She had the illusion that they could sit here, a few feet apart but peacefully close... forever. His eyes were closed, allowing her to watch the deep lines of living on his face as he spoke quietly.

'Robin Conners—his sister Melody writes all his songs. She used to live on the Queen Charlotte Islands—the Misty Isles in the song.'

She loved it when he talked in that lazy voice, the warmth of his words washing over her like happiness. 'Where does she live now?' she asked. She would leave tomorrow, but it would be a long time before she could listen to music again without a feeling of loss.

He said, 'Cortes Island.'

'What?'

His eyes opened and fastened on hers with slow humour. 'You're a long way away tonight, aren't you, Julie?'

She hugged herself, drew her legs up and stared into the flames licking in his big old-fashioned fireplace. 'What about Cortes Island?'

'Conners's sister lives there. She's married to a sea captain. They've got a baby.'

'How do you know that?'

'Mutual friends.'

A songwriter and a sea captain. It might be one of those songs Robin Conners sang in his deep, emotional voice. Love between a man and a woman, a child born of love. Suddenly David's presence seemed so strong to her. She felt yearning swelling up. Not the romantic fantasies of childhood, but a woman's deep need for touching and loving, for belonging in the most elemental way.

She swallowed and jerked to her feet. 'I—er—I'm kind of—I think I'll go to bed.' She got three steps along the front of the sofa, closer to him now, and he wasn't saying a word. She moved to avoid tripping over his long legs. 'Do you want me to...to...?'

She flushed under his dark eyes, grateful for the darkness of the summer night. The late-setting sun had faded to black. There was only the warm flicker of firelight on his face, tones of red and yellow. If he looked, her heated flesh would seem as nothing.

He said, 'You'll need something to sleep in.'

She flushed. Of course he did not mean the words to have the significance her mind had given them, 'No, I-I'll be fine. Goodnight.'

She turned abruptly, disturbed by something in his eyes, terribly afraid that if she did not move she would be closer to him, reaching out to touch his cheek where she could see the shadow of his dark beard.

In her dreams, his lips took hers again. This time there were no barriers, nothing standing between them except the clothes that faded away as he pulled her hard into his arms.

The house was quiet when she woke, the sun blazing through the window, warming her uncomfortably. She lay quietly, listening. In her condominium she could hear the scream of traffic each morning, the roar of the city. Not here. There was a bird somewhere, an eagle screaming into the silence. Then nothing until a cow complained and another answered. A vehicle of some kind, fading to nothing. Julie closed her eyes and heard a woodpecker slowly hammering through the bark of a nearby tree.

When she looked out of the window, she could see the dogwood tree. White flowers, not pink. She had never seen it in bloom, but David had told her about it once, years ago, and she had dreamed it often enough—the new blossoms green and fresh, slowly changing colour from green to yellow to white. Now the flowers were long gone, the tree laden with thick green foliage. She followed the path that ran under the tree with her eyes, from the tree up the hill to the buildings, to a man walking slowly, carrying a full bucket. That must be David's hired hand. When had David woken? Early?

Had he looked in to see her sleeping before he went downstairs?

Of course he hadn't! She knew she was not the woman for a man like David. She knew nothing much about farms and cows, was not particularly interested in learning. She was a city person, using places like Gabriola for holidays. She had none of the virtues a farmer would ask for. There was just this disturbing awareness that had never existed between them before. A sensual pull. Did he feel it too? Would he want——? Oh, God! She had to have some sense! The last thing on this earth that she needed was to be torn apart in an affair that could go nowhere. David as a lover...

She jerked on the robe that she found lying on the cedar chest—a towelling robe, too long for her. It had not been there the night before. David had come in while she slept, must have looked at her sleeping body as he left the robe there for her.

More likely he'd opened the door and dropped the robe on the chest without even looking, without seeing her at all. A good host, doing the right thing. She found bath salts in the bathroom and started to run a deep, hot bath. Then, abruptly, she pulled the plug out. Lying in perfumed luxury while she thought of David outside was more than she could handle this morning. She turned the shower on hard and stepped in, shedding the borrowed robe.

She had not locked the bathroom door!

He would not come in, of course he wouldn't. She was insane, thinking...

She closed her eyes as the water streamed over her hair, her face, down over the fullness of her breasts. David, slipping quietly into the bathroom. David, pulling the curtain back. She would open her eyes and he would be staring at her, his own dark eyes aflame with golden light. Needing her. Reaching for her, the water streaming over their heated flesh, cooling and inflaming and——

She fumbled for the tap, jerked the single control to the right and shuddered as the last of the water trickled down her body. She *must* stop this! What on earth was happening to her? Some kind of hormonal imbalance! Something drastic, and she'd better not let it carry her away. Home—today. Then to the doctor next week for a complete physical. Maybe she was low in iron, her crazy imagination telling her the dizziness was sensual need, when really it was anaemia.

The door. Downstairs, the sound of the door opening, then closing.

She stepped out of the shower, shivering, pulling the towelling robe around her. She pulled a towel off the bar and rubbed the mirror clear until she could see herself in it. Her face was flushed, water balling on her flesh. Her hair was tamed by moisture, hanging in disarray around her face, curling against her neck.

Footsteps, David's boots coming up the stairs. Julie's heart stopped when the sound came closer, along the corridor outside. Then silence, and she closed her eyes. The next thing would be the door opening. She was aching to see him, aching to find again the heat in his eyes that she had seen when she went to bed the night before.

'Julie?'

She dragged in a ragged breath, stared at the closed door. 'Yes?'

'There are fresh eggs in the fridge, and bacon. Or, if you want something lighter, there's yogurt and fruit. Can you manage breakfast on your own? I've got to go over to the feed store.'

She swallowed and said clearly, 'Of course I can manage. What about your breakfast?'

'Already had it.'

So much for the omelette she'd promised him. She felt coolness on her face, the effect of cold water on her fantasies. She picked up a brush and started yanking it through the tangles of her hair. When she heard his footsteps receding, she moved to the door and locked it.

CHAPTER FOUR

SHE was halfway into the borrowed jeans before she realised what she was doing. If she planned to leave today——

Of course she had to leave; David would not welcome her forever. Even more important, she had to get back to reality. The whole notion of coming to Gabriola had been a mistake. She had resisted Wally's urgings over the months and years, had always thought her unwillingness had something to do with not wanting to think too much about the failure of her marriage. The whole thing was just too much a reminder of failure, and who wanted to dwell on failures? She would far rather concentrate on the present, on her teaching and the teenagers she tried to challenge. On the new opportunity to have real input into course development, the chance that she might one day have her own school.

She fastened the waist of the jeans, then slipped on the silk blouse from her suit, adding the big sweatshirt over the blouse.

When the sun came out, she could shed the sweatshirt and feel cool in her blouse. As for the borrowed clothes, she could hardly leave without saying goodbye to David. When he came back from the feed store, she would go and say thanks and sorry about your truck and I think you should put in a claim against me with ICBC, to pay for the damage.

Then she would go over to Sarah's. Jeans would be better for that, too. A white suit was—it wasn't white any more, in any case. The borrowed clothes must be Sarah's anyway, and if she asked she'd be told, of course, keep them as long as you need them.

Borrowed clothes. A tie holding her to Gabriola as long as they were not returned. Borrowed bed. She made it up carefully, leaving no sign that she had been there. Would David look in after she was gone? Would he wish her back?

She was too damned fanciful. She went downstairs to call the insurance people, a conversation that brought her back to cold reality. Whatever David had arranged with the wreckers seemed to have worked, for the car was at the claim centre, awaiting appraisal. She would have to rent a car meanwhile.

'It's going to take a while for repairs,' warned the adjustor. 'Before you go home to Vancouver, you'd better let us know who you want to do the repair work—— Unless we decide to write it off,' added the voice cheerfully. 'We'll pay you out if the estimate is too high.'

She could get a rental car in Nanaimo today, could catch a Vancouver ferry and be back home this afternoon. Back to work on the course development, back to...

She was going to miss David.

'Grow up, Julie,' she muttered, pouring herself a cup of strong coffee from the batch David must have made that morning. She opened the fridge door, then closed it again. Maybe she would eat later. Sarah was bound to offer her lunch. She found a plastic bag in a drawer, took it upstairs and stuffed in her soiled suit and her shoes.

She caught a glimpse of herself in the mirror—jeans and sweatshirt, borrowed trainers. Who owned the trainers? Too small for David, too large for Sarah. Sarah's hand-me-down jeans looked casual and young and relaxed, the oversized sweatshirt something a teenager might wear. She stared at herself and decided that the image did not fit the Julie she had become. Over the years she had slowly let her work image flow into her whole life. Tailored trousers and expensive tops for leisure, suits for work.

She called Sarah before she went looking for David.

Her old friend's voice was warm and excited, the sound of a baby crying in the background. 'Julie! Here on Gabriola? You'd better get over here for a visit before you leave! Can't you stay a few——? No, I'll save that for when you get here. Do you need a ride over from your place?'

'No, I—I'm at David's. I can walk over.'

'David's?' Sarah sounded astounded. 'Well, get him to bring you over. He can spare time from his bloody cows for that, can't he? Tell him if he doesn't, I'll make him baby-sit for us while we take a runaway holiday to Hawaii!'

'I'll tell him,' she promised.

Sarah laughed. 'You never did hesitate to do battle with David. More courage than I've got, I can tell you. He'd not mind looking after the kids anyway, but if you threaten to load my b&b guests on him, he'll smarten up. How on earth did you land up *there*? You two were always at each other's throats.'

'It hasn't changed much,' said Julie wryly, watching the truck drive past the house. As she had expected, David didn't stop, but headed towards the buildings down in the hollow below the farmhouse. 'I'll see you soon, Sarah.'

'Bring some eggs, would you? I've got a whole family of three-eggs-for-breakfast fanatics staying here right now.'

'OK, I will.'

Julie went outside before David could come looking for her. She was a guest, and he had always done the right thing, so he would come soon. Better to meet him outside, amid fresh air and farm smells. She pushed her hands into the back pockets of Sarah's jeans and kept her eyes on her feet as she walked down towards the collection of buildings. She walked along the outside of a wooden fence, wondering if this was the corral where David had been attacked by a young bull. Strange that she had learned nothing about farming all those summers when she was a child. Perhaps not so strange, really. She had never really belonged, just one of the summer people living down by the beach.

She stopped when she saw him. He was coming out of a small building with a mongrel dog at his heels. He smiled when he saw her, the lines at the corners of his eyes crinkling against the sun. 'Sleep well?' he asked.

'Yes, thanks.' She went to the fence, curved her hands around the top rail and stared at the cow on the other side. 'Did you run out of some kind of feed? Chickens?'

David leaned against the fence beside her, his hand absently scratching the dog's ear. 'Dog food,' he corrected. 'We get in chicken feed about once a year, always have a good stock. I should do the same for old Charley here, but I never do. Always run out before I think of it.'

The dog rubbed against Julie's leg, and she reached down to copy David's caress of the floppy ears. She was glad she hadn't worn the white suit. City girl. She could almost hear David's laughter if he knew her thoughts. She asked, 'Is Charley a farm dog? A working dog?'

He chuckled. 'Not likely! The only thing he's good for is watchdog, and that only for strangers who don't know him. He barks, though; keeps the hikers from invading during the tourist season. Did you get breakfast?'

'Coffee. I wasn't hungry.' The dog pressed his head against her knee, asking her not to stop scratching behind his ear.

'You should have something to eat.'

'Telling me what to do again?' She challenged him with her eyes. 'Why do you always do that?'

He shrugged. 'If you'd look after yourself better, I might not feel the urge.'

She frowned at the cow on the other side of that fence. The bovine creature swung its head and stared at them. Julie said pensively, 'This is all you ever wanted to do, isn't it?'

He braced one foot on the bottom rail of the fence. 'I always liked it,' he agreed. 'The island, the variety. I'd have gone nuts in an office job like Patrick's.'

She could see the deep lines carved on his face by the weather. He was a little too rugged to be called handsome, but he was a man people noticed, a man who took charge when something needed doing. Strong jaw, dark brows, dark eyes. A man people counted on, a man who loved his family, looked after them. She did not like to think of him living here alone, but had no words to say what she felt. It was not her place, had never been hers.

'What are you thinking?'

She shrugged.

She saw the smile in his eyes. 'Do you want me to tell you about the cows?'

She laughed and shook her head. 'After all those summers when I avoided learning about them?'

'Did you?' His voice was almost whimsical.

Julie stared at him, breathless excitement beginning to surge through her veins. 'I'll tell you a secret.' Her voice dropped to a whisper. 'They terrify me—they always did scare me. They're so big!'

'That's the first time I've ever heard you admit to being afraid.' He reached over to brush a strand of her hair back behind her shoulder. 'When I hauled you out of the bull pen, you were screaming at me to leave you alone.'

She shook her head, her fingers playing with a splinter of wood on the fence post. 'It was all face-saving. Pat said I was scared and I had to——'

'Prove he was wrong?'

She nodded and met his eyes; was frozen by what she saw there.

'Julie?' His voice was a whisper.

'What?' She felt her fingers curl in on themselves as she stared at the golden light flashing in his dark eyes.

'Come here, Julie.'

Was his voice hoarse? Or was it *her* ears distorting everything? She could not move away, could not seem to come closer. She was frozen, staring, her hazel eyes wide and green-tinged, her trembling lips parted.

He touched her clenched hand, closed his fingers around her wrist. 'Come here,' he said again, pulling gently to bring her into his arms.

Hard muscles, warm embrace. She licked her lips, stared up at his dark gaze, could not look away. His eyes narrowed to golden slits as he bent closer. She could see the deep cleft in his chin, wanted to touch the lines of his forehead, to smooth them away.

'Relax,' he said roughly.

A spasm of trembling surged through her body, then she was pressed hard against him, her soft breasts crushed against his chest.

Relax? When her heart was stopped, his breath on her lips? Her pulse wild and raging?

'Yes,' he whispered as he took her lips.

She had never dreamed his touch would be gentle; but his lips brushed hers lightly, sensuously, taking sweetness and leaving trembling passion. Her hands were spread wide against his chest, his heart beating strongly against her palms.

'So sweet,' he murmured against her lips. He turned and leaned against the fence, bringing her more closely against his hard body. She was resting between his muscular thighs, breathless, staring up wide-eyed. He murmured roughly, 'Do you know I dreamed this? You in my arms.'

His hands hardened across her back, pressing her more intimately against him. She gasped against his open mouth, feeling his body hard against hers. His hands caressed, found the slender curve of her back through the loose shirt, searched gently, discovering... shaping her bodice.

'David...'

He took her parted lips, sought deeper, took what she gave before she knew she had opened to him. She felt his heart hammering under her hands, her breasts crushed between the backs of her own hands and her rib-cage. She could feel their softness swelling, aching for his touch. She pushed her hands against his chest to ease the pressure on her swollen breasts. Her movement brought her hips intimately into the cradle of his thighs, and he took her gasp into his mouth.

His mouth left hers, lips caressing her cheek. 'David—David, do we know what we're...? We shouldn't...'

His mouth silenced her protest. His shoulder, hard under her fingers. Stars spinning out of control. Under her restless fingers, the corded muscle that led to his throat, then back to his neck. David's hand caressing her back, sliding down to the narrow small of her back. His fingers spread wide, possessing her, bringing her closer, curving to possess her hips.

Pulsing heat. Dizzy, spinning, wild images growing, heart pounding. She could feel his need for her, straining, pressing intimately.

'Soft,' he groaned against her throat. 'So soft—haunting me. Dreams.' His lips found hers again and she opened to his invasion. He plundered the softness of her mouth, his tongue thrusting to take possession of the dark secrets of her woman's heat.

A sound, low and wild, blood pounding in her veins. Her flesh, seeking against his in a shattering symbolism of the ultimate possession. His body answering, demanding, arms pulling her closer.

'I don't believe it! What the hell——?'

She felt tension jerk through David. The voice, shocked and young. Julie had heard the words, the strange voice, but they took a moment to penetrate. Her mind was attuned to the man holding her in his arms, to the sound of his breath against her face, the touch of his mouth on hers, the stirring movement of his hand against the small of her back. Wild warmth. With the hard pressure of David's response against her, she had no doubt at all how deeply he desired her.

The voice shattered it—young, angry, shocked. David's hands tensed on her hips, forced her to stillness. She dragged her eyes open. David was staring at something behind her. Someone.

'I don't believe it! Right out in the middle of the bloody—— My own damned father! In broad daylight! Dad, how the hell could you?'

She could see David's eyes, not on her, but on something behind her. Not angry. He would be thinking first, before he said anything. Damn David! Even in the heat of passion, he could stop to think first.

She pulled away, and turned to face the young voice. She remembered him as a small boy, thin and wide-eyed. Stanley. He was older now, as tall as David, rapidly filling out with the gauntness of youth. He looked shatteringly like his father.

Her voice, thank heavens, was clear. 'Hello, Stanley. It's been a long time.'

The boy said nothing, his eyes faltering between anger and confusion. Julie stepped away from David.

'It's nice to see you again, Stanley.' Somehow she manufactured a smile to match the coolness of her voice. This situation had never turned up in any etiquette book she had ever read. She drew in a deep breath and brought her shoulders back stiffly. 'I don't know if you remember me? Julie Summerton. I used to stay in the summer house over on Mountainview Lane.'

She nodded towards Stanley, as if he were one of her students met on a downtown street, then she got her legs moving. She did not let herself look at David, would not look at either the man or his son. Somehow she got to the house. Inside David's kitchen, she leaned back against the door and closed her eyes.

Stanley didn't believe it? That was nothing to the feelings raging inside her. Julie shuddered, overcome by echoes of sensation. A kiss, David's hardness pressed against her, her own flesh welcoming his need as a drowning person must gulp for air. Just touches, kisses, but the shattering intimacy of it would be with her forever.

She shivered, disorientated, torn away from the edge of need. With her eyes closed, his arms were around her again. Madness, that was what it had been. Heaven knew why he had done that, pulling her close and kissing her as if he could not penetrate her soul deeply enough for his need. Making her need him in ways that would haunt her for the rest of her life.

Her fingers curled in on themselves. What was he telling his son? Stanley had been so shocked that this must never have happened before. Was she the first woman in David's arms since Sandy's death? Or just the first Stanley knew about?

She shuddered under the echo of passion. Face it, it wasn't Julie who had David in that state. Three years since his wife's death, and David was a normal man. But in those three years if he'd been alone—— Any woman would have got the same reaction. She must have come along at just the right moment.

The wrong moment.

*   *   *

She was halfway down the steps from the veranda when he strode up to her. She had hoped for a few more minutes. She had looked out of the window, had seen David and Stanley down by the corral, talking—angrily, she thought, and that bothered her.

David's kiss bothered her more. It was past time for her to go. Julie had admitted that to herself as she dashed up and retrieved the plastic bag filled with her clothes. She had her bag, her clothes. She raced back down—front door, veranda. Down one step, then she came to a screeching halt.

David, staring up at her.

'Running away?' he asked grimly.

'Going back where I belong,' she said flatly. 'I should have gone sooner.'

He pushed his hands into the pockets of his jeans. 'Don't leave, Julie.'

Her heart stopped, but there was nothing in his eyes, only the mask that could hide anything at all. Behind David, she could see Stanley watching from the fence down the hill. Watching, knowing she did not belong, waiting for her to leave.

'Why?' she asked in a choked voice. 'Why should I stay?'

'You know damned well why.'

'What do you want?' she demanded tightly. 'A one-night stand? With me?'

'Don't be a damned fool!' he snapped. 'Stanley's just a boy, upset because—— Don't let it get to you.'

'Get to me?' She heard her voice rising, bit down and rammed her free hand into Sarah's jeans pocket. 'Get out of my way and let me go!'

'Julie, you're not being rational.'

She made herself focus on a cow out in the field. 'This—it should never have happened. You never approved of me. All my life, you've disapproved of the way I've done things, of me. You don't know anything about me. How can you——?' She closed her eyes, thinking of Stanley. 'He's right, you know. I don't belong here, with you. I can't even imagine how...' She shivered, the touch of his fingers hot on her mind. 'It wasn't me. It wasn't you. And I'm leaving.'

He grasped her wrist as she began to move, and she stared at the fingers of his dark, tanned hand. She said dully, 'You're just...getting carried away by the...the heat of the... Can you imagine us? You and I. We're the last two people in the world who could ever——' It was true, but it hurt to say it. She shook her head, tried to keep the tears back. When she pulled, he let her wrist free.

She said in a stilted voice, 'I'm not into meaningless relationships. And you—— I—— Oh, hell!' Stay, he had said. But he was not asking again now. An impulse? An attempt to make up for Stanley's rude interruption? 'Let me go,' she muttered, but he was not holding her. She backed up, away from him. 'I'm going to Sarah's. Before I...leave.'

'I'll drive you.'

'No, I'd rather walk.'

She had to walk past the fence where Stanley was sitting to get to the road. She did not know what to say to the boy; she wanted to say something, but there were no words. Stanley slid off the fence and stopped her progress along the drive.

He growled, 'Look, I—— Sorry. It was none of my business.'

David's words on Stanley's lips, she supposed. 'Forget it,' she said wearily. 'But don't wish a life of solitude on your father, just because you can't face seeing another woman in his arms.'

She heard the engine behind her. David at the wheel of a small blue pick-up truck. He pulled up beside her. 'Get in,' he said abruptly.

She could see the scene if she refused. Herself walking down the drive, David following, bull-headed and determined she would get in. He would follow all the way to Sarah's if he had to.

She jerked the door of the truck open. 'You always had to have the last word, didn't you?'

'If possible,' he agreed.

That was the last thing he said all the way to Sarah's place. He pulled up in front of the rambling house and jerked the brake on. Julie got out, muttered, 'Thanks for the ride,' and he reversed and roared away down the drive.

Then Sarah was running out, her straight black hair swinging as she threw her arms around Julie and said with suppressed laughter, 'What did you do to David? He looked furious—did you bring the eggs?'

CHAPTER FIVE

JULIE had one of Sarah's babies in her arms when Edward's pager sounded. The other twin was lying on the sofa beside her, gurgling around its fist. When the pager sounded, everything fell silent, just the echo of a mechanical voice with a crackle of static filling the kitchen.

'Brush fire reported on Gabriola Island, South Road.'

Edward dropped the chopping knife on the vegetable block.

Sarah said, 'Take the wagon. Your gear is in the back.'

'Right,' he said, bending to brush a kiss on her lips.

'And be careful!' called Sarah as he went out.

Julie hugged the baby close to her chest. 'Edward's a volunteer fireman?' She had forgotten until now that Gabriola was served by a volunteer fire department. After the highly organised life of Vancouver, it seemed odd and very rural.

Sarah nodded. 'Yes. So's David. Pat too, but he's away.'

Julie closed her eyes. 'Is it dangerous?'

'They're careful. They're trained to be careful, but...' Sarah shrugged. 'David says I worry too much.'

Julie bounced the baby on her knee and wondered if she was holding Terry or Tammy. She would know as soon as she went to change the baby's nappy. Six-year-old Sally came through the back door and settled on the sofa beside Julie.

'My daddy's goin' to a fire. My daddy's a fireman...an' Uncle David's a captain. Did you know that?'

Julie found her hand going to Sally's soft, fair hair. 'Your mommy told me. You must be proud of them.'

Sally bounced. 'They fought the Olsen fire, you know. The house would have burned to the ground if it weren't for the firem'n. I'm gonna be a fireman when I grow up.'

'Firefighter,' corrected Sarah automatically. 'You can't be a *fireman*.' She turned to the chopping block and carried on with Edward's salad.

'Can I help with the dinner?' asked Julie.

Sarah shook her head. 'Just keep an eye on the twin terrors for me. If they start hassling me, dinner will be hours late.'

Waiting. It seemed forever. She would remember this back in Vancouver. She would listen to the news, but she doubted that a fire on Gabriola would make headlines in the city. Be careful, Sarah had warned her husband. Burning buildings, trees falling to the ground in flames. Julie tried to suppress the images of David flashing in front of her eyes. David, caught in a fire. David, trapped and burning. David...

Julie helped Sarah serve dinner for the guests out in the dining-room. The murmur of conversation, a loud voice telling Sarah she was a *bonnie* cook. Back in the kitchen, Sarah and Julie picked at their own meal while Sally chattered about fires and wished her brother Jeremy were back from summer camp.

Then Edward was back, the crunch of wheels on the gravel outside. Sarah ran out to the car, leaving the door swinging wide behind her. Edward was dodging her embrace as they came into the kitchen, laughing and warning, 'Don't touch me, love—I'm all soot and mess. What a bloody job!'

'Did you get it out?'

'Oh, yeah, but it was a close thing.' His thin face strained into worry lines that seemed habitual. 'That section of bush is a tinderbox this time of year. Had to make a fire wall, digging in the debris and dirt, but in the end we got it out with the hoses. We figure some idiot threw a cigarette into the brush.'

'David?' Julie's voice was cracked.

'He was there too. He's captain of the fire hall at this end,' explained Edward. 'Like me, he's all soot and mess. Gone home to clean up, I imagine. He might stop by later.'

Julie knew that she should leave now, go to her own cottage and spend the night with the old cobwebs. Better still, she should leave the island, catch the last ferry to Nanaimo.

But Sarah had asked her to stay.

Running? echoed David's voice. Make up your mind.

Sarah let Julie put the twins to bed. Julie hugged little Tammy close before laying her down. Terry, she had realised, was all elbows and knees, not a cuddly baby. But Tammy...

He was there when she came back downstairs, standing in the kitchen. She tried to walk in as if he were not there, to ignore his eyes on her. Impossible with her heart thudding harshly against her rib-cage and Sarah watching with curiosity wild in her eyes.

'Come outside,' said David abruptly. 'I have to talk to you.'

Julie shook her head.

Sarah said, 'David, have you eaten supper yet?'

He ignored the question and walked slowly across the open space between himself and Julie. She should move...she could not move. Her heart stilled, waiting, her breath frozen in her lungs. He reached out and took her hand. She told herself she should pull away, shout at him, scream something to stop him grabbing her and pulling her where he wanted her to go. She stared at him, her legs moving as he led her outside. Sarah and Edward watching, silent. Behind them, Sally, demanding loudly, 'Uncle David? Was it a good fire?'

Outside, he released her. She moved away from him, towards the trees, away from the house. She stopped and stared at her wrist where there was a faint shadow from his grip. 'You're making a habit of that,' she said unevenly. 'Dragging me around as if I were a child.' She sucked in a noisy gulp of air. 'What do you imagine Sarah and Edward think?'

He said nothing, just his eyes watching her. She felt the contrast—her own rising voice, David's silence. He would win with the silence. But win what?

She gulped. 'You can't just burst in and drag off your sister's guests.'

'I did.' Was he laughing at her?

Nothing had happened. A kiss. His arms holding her. Whoever heard of a woman making a scene over a kiss these days? It would be nothing, a pinprick of irritation, except that...

She moved away and kept moving, unable to turn and look at him, then stopped finally by the pond in her path. She stared down at the mottled grey duck swimming quietly amid its own ripples.

'Julie——'

She moved abruptly, swung away when she felt him close. She hated the restlessness surging through her. She might say anything, do anything, with this wildness in her veins. She needed desperately to get away from him, yet she knew she could not go back into the house where Sarah would stare at her flushed face.

'Julie, stop wasting all that energy.'

She had not meant to swing around, to let her eyes be locked on him. David. So still, such a contrast to the trembling nervousness surging through her. 'Why did you come? Why not simply let me go home?'

His eyes changed. 'Home?' He moved and she was frozen, helpless before his touch. His hands on her shoulders, fingers pressing her close. Her body impacting softly against his, lips open.

'This,' he said roughly, covering her open mouth with his. 'I had to know if this was real.'

She told herself to feel anger, to push him away, but when he spread his hands out across her back, she felt herself softening, clinging to the hard warmth of his man's body against hers. His lips, his tongue, the groan of his harsh voice, whispered words. 'Haunting me! I dream your skin under my fingers...wake up with your mouth, lips parted under mine...dream when I'm not even sleeping.' He took her mouth in a deep, plundering kiss, demanded raggedly, 'What the hell are you doing to me, Julie? Why?'

She pulled back. He released her, but she could not walk away. His eyes, probing hers. Her own heart reaching, anything but cool.

Weak, boiling underneath, nervous with...
desire.

She whispered, 'It's not—I—we can't
just...it's some kind of insanity and...and
it'll be gone once...'

He did not hold his hand out to her, but
his eyes would not let her free. No words
spoken, but she felt the power of him drawing
her, whispered, 'We can't. We... This is insanity! If we...you...I don't——' She
trembled, knew she must walk back into
Sarah's house now if she was to avoid being
destroyed by what was inside her.

Something snapped in him. She felt it, and
knew she should run. Then he was pulling her
roughly closer, his hands gentling as her body
joined his. Softly he stroked her cheeks, the
side of her neck. She heard the sound of her
own breath leaving her lungs. 'You—you've
got to let me go!'

'No.' His lips sought her trembling mouth.
'If you wanted free, you'd fight me. You've
never hesitated to fight before.'

'Can't,' she whispered, but there was no
sound. Everything in her heart reaching for
him, her mind screaming as he traced her ear
with his mouth, tasted the tender flesh at the
side of her throat.

His voice, murmuring, 'I dreamed you last night, going mad, knowing you were just down the hall...knowing you'd refused something to sleep in...knowing you were lying naked under the sheets. I dreamed you were waiting for me.' She shuddered and he said harshly, 'I should have come to you then.'

'It's crazy. We're...not rational.' She had worshipped him as a child, but never this wild and overwhelming need.

He laughed, his lips seeking the trembling softness of her throat. 'Aren't you the girl who leaps in without looking first?'

'Not this.' Julie was frightened, could feel how little control she had over what was happening...the magnetism this man's touch had for her. 'We can't—— Stanley's right.'

Can't. She kept saying the same words over and over, but his hand drifted down her back until he found her hip, then he brought her close against him. She gasped softly.

David said in a low voice, 'You don't want me to stop. I can feel it when I'm near you. What I feel—what I need—— It's not just me.'

He grasped her hands and placed them on his chest, where they became restless, worrying at the abrasion of his hair through the

thin shirt, the ridges of his muscles. She heard
a sound like a groan, then his lips took hers,
hard and hungry. 'Come with me, Julie.'

'We can't,' she whispered.

'Come for a walk, then.' She pulled back
and he said slowly, 'Are you afraid, Julie?'

Yes. God, she was terrified!

'A walk through the trees,' he said softly,
his voice suddenly gentle. 'What's to run
from?'

Everything. The need raging in her. The
hunger she had felt when he touched her. Now
his eyes were masked and he said in a low,
toneless voice, 'I dare you, Julie. What harm
in twenty minutes' walking?'

'Sarah and Edward. They'll expect me
back.' She sounded like a child, nervous,
uneasy, the situation out of her control.

He said harshly, 'I don't give a damn what
Sarah wants.'

She would be crazy to trust him when he
was like this. There was something in him that
she had never seen before, emotion in his eyes
that was masked from her. David was always
controlled, angry only when he thought she
was being stupid. But now, tonight—— He
held out his hand and she moved with him,

out of the clearing and into a well-worn game trail made by the deer.

'Have you seen the log house beyond Pat's?'

Julie flexed her fingers, but he seemed to have no intention of releasing her hand. She could still feel danger in the air, knew it could abruptly explode. There was steel inside David. Until now, she had not known it could turn molten and dangerous.

'I'll show it to you,' he said, as if she had answered. 'It was built by Jim Oldham. He sold it to Molly's father.'

She tried to make herself breathe normally. It wasn't the walk, she surely could not be that badly out of shape, although he *was* leading her uphill. 'Molly?' she asked desperately. 'You mean Pat's wife?'

'Hm. Her father's an artist, came here and settled in to paint the deer. He stayed six months, then gave the place to Molly.'

'Molly stayed longer?' Her voice sounded almost normal now. She had blown the whole thing out of proportion. Of course David wasn't going to...it was in her mind, wild fantasies. But this was David, and soon they would come to a stump to be stepped over. He would let her hand free. It would be all right then. She would get her breath—in more ways than one. She felt a desperate need for time to get her bearings. Too much, too soon. But it was all in her imagination, wasn't it? He was teasing her. Or——

David didn't tease. Patrick was the tease, but David...

Julie gulped. 'Is she really an artist too? Molly? Dinosaur pictures?'

'Didn't Sally show you the books?'

It was a fallen tree, a big trunk blocking the path. He released her hand and she told herself to turn back, head for Sarah's, but his eyes locked on hers and she knew he would stop her, touch her, pull her into his arms. Behind him, she could see the log walls of the house that belonged to Patrick's wife.

'I'll help you over,' David said.

'We should go back. I...'

He stepped across, turned back and held his hand out for her. The sun was low in the sky, late summer sun, throwing his face into silhouette. She gave him her hand.

He led her towards the cabin.

'We can't go...inside.'

He opened the door. 'Why not?'

She could not seem to do anything but follow him. An open living-room with a cathedral ceiling, an open loft upstairs, log walls. Julie said, 'I smell something like paint.' Her voice sounded hollow, far away.

'Molly's using it for a studio.'

'She won't want us to...'

'She won't mind.'

Julie turned and tried to study a painting on the log wall. Sally and Jeremy, playing in the field with a dinosaur. 'She must have painted this for them.'

'Hm.' She shuddered at the touch of his breath on her neck. Then his lips, brushing against the side of her neck, and he must have felt her trembling.

From behind, his slid his hands down along her arms. Through the thick softness of the sweatshirt she felt his touch like fire. Gently he took her clenched fists in his fingers and prised her fists open. She sighed, almost a groan, as his teeth took gentle possession of her earlobe.

'Please...' she whispered. 'We—can't.'

He stroked her palms with his thumbs, and she felt her own body tremble again, a final protest as her back settled against his chest. He said with harsh gentleness, 'This has been between us from the moment you stared up at me from the seat of your wrecked car.'

'I——'

He turned her in his arms. 'Nothing else can come until this is settled.'

She shook her head silently.

'Just feel,' he said softly. He brought her hands to his chest, took her lips in a long kiss that left her spinning, aching for his touch, his possession. His fingers brushed her throat, then lower. He heard her soft indrawn breath, felt the tension ripple through her.

'Are you shy of me?' he asked wonderingly, drawing her closer. 'My God,' he whispered against her throat, feeling the trembling there. Images. Julie, wild and longing in his arms. The vision made him dizzy with excitement and he murmured, 'I want to see you, touch you. I need to know if you'll cry out when I possess your breast with my mouth. Soft...so soft.'

'David, I-I'm not sure we...'

He could hear beyond her words, knew what would happen if he touched her midriff, moved his lips on her throat in an erotic caress. He had felt the fire in her now, and knew he could stir it again. He felt the soft warmth surging through her as he drew her closer. 'When I touch you...I feel you wanting me.' He kissed the side of her lip, felt her response and nibbled gently. When he felt her hands clench against his chest he reached to close his grip over them.

He pushed her hands flat against the contours of his chest. 'I've dreamed of your softness.' His own palms curved around the slopes of her breasts, brushed gently against nipples that were suddenly hard and rigid.

'What are you going to do?' she whispered in a harsh voice.

He traced his fingers slowly down the side of her throat, came to rest on the pulse that beat wildly in the hollow at the base of her throat. 'I'm going to make love to you,' he said steadily.

Her throat convulsed. 'But I... It...this is a mistake.' She felt the trembling, the frightening need. Was it a dream? A wild fantasy? The whole thing unreal?

His fingers smoothing heated flesh, lips gentle on the pale smoothness of her throat. 'You could say no,' he murmured, covering her mouth with his.

What use to whisper words when his hands slipped under the waistband of the sweatshirt and she melted against him? When he swung her up into his arms, she closed her eyes and the world was all red. Hazy. Hot. Desperate.

Her eyes closed, feeling the movement of his strong body as he climbed the stairs. Upstairs, to the loft. She felt the softness of a mattress at her back, stared up, and there was nothing but the harsh darkness of his eyes, his lips moving to possess.

His hands in her hair, his mouth moving to take hers. She turned molten with need as his touch moved to learn her curves, his thumb brushing across the hard pressure of a nipple through soft fabric. No moon, only the fading day through windows that looked out on the trees. He took the sweatshirt away gently. When he reached the thin, silky blouse underneath, the buttons gave way at his touch. She felt her breath, painful in harsh gulps. When his hands closed on the lacy fabric of her bra, a slow moan escaped her throat.

Somehow she was sitting, facing him on the bed. Molly's bed? She tried to grasp that reality, but David traced a line of fire down her cheek with his index finger. Down to her throat. She felt the muscles turning to spasm as he traced heat along the base of her throat, as his finger slipped under the strap of her bra. He slipped the strap from one shoulder. She heard the whimper, and it could not have been her sound, but the air touched the naked flesh of her breast and his eyes told her that his lips would be there next, that he would draw her into his mouth, his tongue soft and fiery on her.

The other strap. Oh...! She would die with the waiting. His hands, cupping underneath her softness, fingers stretched back, curled around her sides. She felt her own hands settling into his forearms, fingers digging into his flesh. David, bending down, his lips...his mouth taking her softness, suckling, tongue curled to caress the hard peak. Something pulled deep inside her, a fathomless cord of need at her woman's centre. She felt everything slipping away, the madness riding up, taking over. Her voice, crying out his name.

When he moved away from her, she could see nothing but flames, could feel nothing but the hardness of his forearms under her hands, could hear only the harsh echo of her own ragged gulps for air.

'Do you want me to stop?'

His voice was low, eyes holding hers as his hand brushed the place where his lips had suckled only a second ago. Her fingers dug into the hard muscles of his arms. Then he bent to her again, and her body strained against his in primeval need.

*   *   *

Silence. Darkness. Julie closed her eyes, felt the pressure of David's body against hers. Opened them, saw darkness, shadows against darkness. She breathed in slowly and the weight of his hand on her breast grew more. His breathing, soft against her throat.

He was sleeping, holding her close while he breathed slowly against her flesh. She closed her eyes in darkness again, the night without moon or stars. She felt drained, emotion wrung dry from passion. His touch would be with her forever. He had driven her beyond the edge of reason, had taken her body where it had never been, forced her to fulfilment and left her cold and damp, lying in his sleeping arms and knowing that while he had taken a man's pleasure in her driven body, he had done it deliberately.

Every moment, knowing exactly what he was doing...while she lost her mind in his arms.

Her heart hammered as she moved away from his sleeping embrace. She had never felt so cold, so painfully exposed and terrified of daylight. Of David's eyes looking at her, knowing he possessed her. Possession.

She shivered, her feet on the bare wood of the loft floor, her hands fumbling, finding the jeans, the shirt. She could not find her panties or her bra, dared not turn on the light. And the blouse. Where was the thin blouse she'd worn under the sweatshirt?

Oh, God! Forget the damned blouse. This was enough. Anonymous trainers, jeans, sweatshirt. Silently down the stairs, the faint sound of David's breathing. No words of love, just touch and passion and exhaustion. Sex. That was what she had shared with him. Controlled, touching, tantalising, inflaming.

For her. The man who put her out of control of her own world had kept perfect control of his. Damn David!

She froze as the door creaked in her hand, but there was nothing but silence, darkness. She slipped outside, closed the door and stood in total darkness, wondering what she was going to do now. Go back to Sarah's in the dark? Back to curiosity and open stares because she must be flushed with passion, her flesh bearing the musky scent of loving.

Not loving. She stumbled and moved away from the house. There were no stars—an overcast night. There must have been a torch inside that house of Molly's, but she could not bring herself to go back inside. David had been curled against her, his big body relaxed and almost vulnerable in complete sleep, but if she went back, he might wake. God knew what difference it made now, but she could not face him. Never again.

There was no reason on earth why she had to see David again. She would walk to the ferry terminal. Lord, it must be ten or twelve kilometres, but that was the only thing she could do. The middle of the night. She had no idea what time it was; she lifted her wrist and tried to see her watch, but the light glared at her when she pushed the button, somehow making it impossible to read the numbers. Two o'clock? Could it be that late?

That early?

The first ferry would not leave until six in the morning.

Her bag was at Sarah's. Julie swallowed and faced a wall of dark shadows—trees. The path, but she would never find it in the dark. There was the driveway down to McNaughton Road, not lit either, but at least a lighter shadow against the darkness of the trees.

It took forever, stumbling along the uneven gravel of Molly's driveway. Julie didn't realise when she got to the road, somehow got off the track, stumbled on the edge of the drainage culvert and barely escaped falling into the ditch.

'Just great,' she muttered, turning left and hoping she'd stay on the damned road in the dark. Now her eyes were adjusting better, she could see the edges of the road, or the beginning of the darkness that was trees. She gritted her teeth and stayed in the middle, wondering what she would do if a car came, wondering why on earth a car would come up here in the middle of the night.

There was a light shining down the next drive. Patrick's house. He'd installed a solar switch in his yard light years ago. One more drive and it would be Sarah's. Yes, there it was. The bed and breakfast sign was illuminated. Julie turned and walked along the drive. It was smoother than Molly's, recently graded. She tried to move silently, certain that the crunch of gravel under her borrowed running shoes would wake everyone in the house, guests and family alike.

What if David was there? He might have woken when she left, slipped out of Molly's cabin and come silently through the trees. Waiting for her at Sarah's, waiting... He wasn't there. Why should he be? He'd got what he wanted, a one-night stand, and she

had nothing now, just the emptiness of fulfilment haunted by the knowledge that David
had taken her without love. He had known
he could make her forget her protests. His
touch had been gentle, arousing, might have
seemed loving if she had not known that his
heart was nowhere near his actions.

She circled the house, going to the kitchen
door. She did not want to wake anyone, and
she knew that there were creaking boards in
the front corridor that would bring Sarah or
Edward investigating. Thank goodness hardly
anyone locked a door here on Gabriola.

The kitchen was lit with ghostly illumi-
nation from a small night light on the counter.
Julie leaned against the door, breathing
gently, trying to still her heart. He wasn't here.
Of course he wasn't, and David would never
make a scene in his sister's sleeping house.
When he did wake, he would go home, come
back in the morning for the truck parked by
Sarah's back door.

Her handbag was on a shelf in the family
room, where Sarah had put it hours earlier.
Julie picked it up and tiptoed back outside.
She should leave a note for Sarah, some kind
of apology, but she could not make herself go
back inside. Any minute David might come.

Her heart was hammering slowly and nervously as she stood alone outside. She could go to her cottage, stand shivering in the darkness and wait for him to come. He might not come looking for her tonight, but she knew David. Morning would come, and he would make sure she was all right. He would find her, make sure she had a ride to the ferry.

Make sure there were no repercussions from what had happened in Molly's empty cabin, because if there had been precautions taken the night before, she had no memory of...

He had—of course he had. David did everything deliberately, doing what he planned and pushing it aside if it wasn't in the plan. God help Sandy, who had been pregnant when David married her, if it hadn't been in his plan. She trembled and knew that was wrong, that David always took the consequences of his actions. Julie was the one who always ran away. He'd accused her of that once, and she was proving it tonight. But she was damned if she'd wait for him to drive her to the ferry in the morning. Damned if——

Everything had to be David's way, ever since she was a small child worshipping him during her summers. Not this time. Tonight it would be Julie's way, and the next time—

if she ever saw him again, it would be on her terms. And her terms were never. Not ever. Again.

In typical Gabriolan style, David had left his keys in the ignition of the little truck. She opened the door and slid into the driver's seat. He would be furious. She knew that, but somehow it no longer mattered. When she started the engine, a light came on at the back of the house.

Sarah and Edward's room.

Julie shifted into gear and put the headlights on. She was tensed, ready for that kitchen door to open and someone to come out asking what the hell was going on, but the house remained silent. As she put the truck in gear and moved slowly down the drive, the light went back out.

'None of our business,' Edward would be telling Sarah. Sarah would agree, but she would be raging with curiosity. Julie and David. They had argued and shouted all through Julie's childhood. Actually, Julie had done most of the shouting. David's words had mostly been spoken with quiet harshness, telling her what a fool she was, lecturing her as if he were her older brother instead of...

She supposed David would always be Sandy's husband. Sandy, alive in his heart. That was why he had taken her body without giving her even the smallest part of his heart.

She shifted into second gear as she turned on to McNaughton Road, then third as she barrelled past the farm. Was Stanley there, wondering where his father was? Would David get a lecture from his son when he got home? Serve him right if he did.

She would drop him a postcard, saying 'Thanks for the hospitality', and he would wonder just what she really meant.

She wouldn't, of course she wouldn't. She would send a note to Sarah, though. Lord knew what words she could put in it, but something. Sorry, I didn't mean to fall in love with your brother. I—— She was *not* in love with David! Hero-worship from all those years ago, and how could a woman resist the man who had been her first love? It *wasn't* love. If nothing else, David had given her the complete cure for...whatever it was.

She jammed the gearshift roughly back into second for the turn on to North Road. Not love, and of course she would not be pregnant. How could she be? It wasn't the right time. She was sure it was safe, and David must have taken precautions. He was always cautious. Always—never impulsive, so it hadn't been an impulse. Deliberate. He had known when he led her out of Sarah's exactly where he would take her, exactly what he would do when he got her there. He had known, planned, known even then that she would not be able to resist if he touched her just so, caressed her to stir the madness.

She was *not* going to cry. She would leave his truck at the ferry terminal. Maybe she would leave a note in it. Thanks for the loan of your truck. Leave the keys in it.

The terminal was dark and empty. She parked, got out and walked to the sign. Same sign, same schedule. The first ferry left at six. It was three o'clock now. Three hours. Would he come? In the big dump truck? Or in Sarah's station wagon? He might. Checking on her, to make sure she was all right. Bawling her out because it had been stupid to run off like that. What was the big deal? She was a grown woman, wasn't she? And——

She got back into the truck and started it. She would go to Gabriola Sands park, walk on the beach, kill time. Then, when the ferry came—— It would serve David right if she took his truck all the way to Vancouver. Inconsiderate, but he hadn't stopped to think about her, had he? Not last night, pulling her into his arms, telling her he knew she could not resist, did not *want* to resist. He might say that Tom had taken advantage of Julie back when she was seventeen, but David——

He must have known, all these years, that he had a place in her heart. But it had been a child's place. He had no right to use her childish love as a tool to take her woman's body.

CHAPTER SIX

SAMUEL, six feet one and dreadfully thin, shook back shaggy hair and declared heatedly, 'The play wasn't the way to do it. Hamlet should have known it was a fool scheme.'

Ellie, six inches shorter and angry, growled. 'You're wrong. The play was a good idea. If he could have just made up his mind after and faced down Claudius.'

Samuel retaliated, 'Or killed him in the first place, when his father told him he'd been murdered.'

Warren, usually silent, said, 'Don't be a twit, Sam. Would you go kill Ms Summerton if some ghost came and told you she was guilty of murder?'

Samuel, who had a crush on his teacher, flushed vividly.

Julie was perched on the side of her desk with one leg swinging as she watched. She decided it was time to interrupt. 'All right, then. What should Hamlet have done? Where did he go wrong?'

Fifteen different answers came to her. Trust Hamlet's indecisive behaviour to get a new class loosened up! 'OK,' she said cheerfully. 'I can't hear all of you at once. Tell it to me on paper. Seven hundred words or more, due a week from next Thursday. How would you have done it, if you were Shakespeare?'

Ellie dropped her wildly gesticulating hands in disgust. 'Thanks a lot, Sam, you got us into this one.'

Warren mused, 'Why don't we re-write the whole thing? Could we, Ms Summerton? We could put it on for the Christmas concert. That would give my dad a jolt. The gospel of Shakespeare according to the kids!'

The bell rang and they moved out of the room in a noisy cloud of laughter. Julie bent over her books and started tidying the chaos of the day. So far, her approach to Shakespeare for the grade twelves was going well, although the Principal had been sceptical. She smiled, wishing Dev Harrington could be in the corridor right now, listening to the excited cacophony outside her room. They were still arguing about whether Hamlet was a fool or simply too cautious.

'Interesting,' said a quiet voice. The voice from her dreams.

She froze, her fingers tightening on the papers.

He was there in the far doorway, leaning against the frame as if he'd been there for hours. How long? Heaven knew. She'd been so wrapped up in driving the class into controversy over *Hamlet* that the roof could have fallen in and she wouldn't have noticed.

'Were you looking for a class in Shakespeare?' She was proud of her voice, cool and uninterested. What was he doing wearing city clothes?

'I thought they had rows in classrooms.' He started threading his way through the chairs strewn around the room.

'Old-fashioned.' She was very aware of the breadth of his shoulders, the way he looked in a sports jacket and tailored trousers. She had seen him dressed that way perhaps four times in her life. He'd always seemed foreign to her in city clothes. Good, she thought. Her turf, her home territory. He would be the one at a disadvantage this time. She said in a lecture-voice, 'Shoulder-to-shoulder learning doesn't stimulate the intellect, it stifles it. They should communicate with each other, not just listen to teacher like a bunch of empty vessels waiting to be filled with knowledge.'

David leaned on a table a couple of feet away from her, crossing his arms and looking as if he would be there hours from now, or next week. Julie piled the tests from this morning on top of the photocopies of an article for the advertising class, then dumped a volume of Shakespeare's complete works on top.

'This is a school, David. If it's not Shakespeare you came for, then what?'

'The teacher.'

Her eyes lifted to meet his. Ice to ice. She said quietly, 'Wasn't once enough?'

'No,' he answered, equally tonelessly.

She studied his eyes, his face. Hard. He was a hard man. She had never realised that before, had thought humour and warmth in his eyes said something about what was inside. 'Too bad,' she said coldly, 'because that's all you're going to get.'

The door burst open and a lean, leggy blonde rushed in, spotted David and froze. 'Sorry, Julie, I didn't realise you had a parent in here.' The blonde backed up a few feet, said, 'Catch me before you go, will you?'

Julie said, 'Hold on, Emily. I'll come with you.'

The woman froze in mid-retreat. 'But——'

'Mr McNaughton's just leaving.' Julie gave David a nod of dismissal. She walked out of her room first, leaving him to follow. He might not go if she waited, willing him to leave.

Why was he here? Surely he would not make a scene. Not David.

He might. That look in his eyes——

'Staff-room?' she muttered to Emily, knowing David's eyes were still on her.

Inside the staff-room, Emily hissed, 'Julie, who is he? You surely wouldn't talk to a parent like that? You sounded——'

'He's not that kind of parent.'

Emily shook back her hair, worried. 'If he's a parent, he'll be complaining to Dev, and you'll be on the carpet. That man is *not* the type to let you get away with being snotty.'

Julie said curtly, 'He's not one of my parents. He—— You know what I mean.'

'No, I don't.' Emily's eyes narrowed. 'You're being remarkably confusing for someone who teaches the English language.'

Julie moved to the coffee-pot and poured herself a cup.

Emily warned 'That's foul coffee, I wouldn't drink it. You mean, he's a *man*?'

Julie shrugged.

'You? With a man?' Emily sat down abruptly. 'I don't believe it.'

Julie said wryly, 'It's been known. I used to date your husband, if you'll remember.'

Emily laughed. 'Sure, and when I stole him from you you wished us every happiness. When I say *man*, I mean—this is different. Look at you!'

'What about me?' Julie had wanted there to be nothing that showed.

'No smile, no frown. That's not exactly the Julie we know around here. Where's all that emotion, passion——?' Emily laughed and said, 'Don't climb all over me! I mean passion in a sense of emotional excess, not...well, not the classic man-woman kind. At least—face it, when were you ever silenced by a mere man?'

Julie shook her hair back and closed her eyes. 'Would you check if he's still out there?'

Emily's brows shot up. 'What if he is?'

'Then walk me to my car?'

'Oh, brother! You've got it bad, girl!'

Julie snapped, 'I haven't got anything. Just—just take a look, would you? And if you won't walk me out, could you get my stack of things from my room?'

'You're going to sit here on a Friday afternoon and do marking while he waits for you to come out?'

Julie spun around. 'What am I supposed to do? I don't want to talk to him. I don't want to see him. He won't go away until I come out. I know him, damn it! He'll sit out there for a month if he's got some damned...'

Her friend touched her shoulder. 'Cool down, honey. I'll call Allan, and he'll come pick us up.'

'Like a bloody wimp,' muttered Julie. 'Why am I letting him do this to me?'

'Why don't you just talk to him?' suggested Emily rationally.

Julie squeezed her eyes tightly closed. 'You don't *talk* to David. At least, *I* don't. Shout at him! Scream at him! Nothing makes any difference.'

'This isn't a new man?' Emily glanced at the door uneasily. 'Is this the infamous Mr Summerton? Your ex?'

Julie almost laughed. 'No, it isn't. If it were Tom, it wouldn't matter. Will you look?'

The door to the corridor opened. Both women tensed, then relaxed when they saw

Dev's lean form. The Principal fixed intense grey eyes on them. 'What's up? Friday afternoon and you're still here?'

'Discussing curriculum,' lied Emily, glancing at Julie.

'Hm.' Dev's face moved from curious to professional. 'Julie, I'll have to give you one. That new-wave Shakespeare thing is a massive hit.'

'Thanks.' Her voice sounded slightly hoarse. She smiled, to take the sudden curiosity out of Dev's eyes. He was too observant. He'd been known to single an anonymous student out of a crowd and drag him into the office, digging out problems that no one else had dreamed were hidden under a teenaged face.

'I—I think I'll head off,' she said uneasily. She had to be a flaming wimp to be shivering in the staff-room, afraid to face a mere man.

'Past time,' said Dev, watching her with that sudden intensity.

She moved towards the door, tried to walk as she would normally, didn't know how that was, but could feel her legs moving as if through heavy water.

When had she ever hidden from David before? Never, but this was different. Or was it? It had always been a battle for control, but, until last month, she hadn't lost any of the rounds.

'Round one to the contender,' she muttered. 'But the war is going to go to me.'

'What?' demanded Dev.

'A new play,' said Emily quickly. 'Julie's been going over her drama students' outlines. Some of them are pretty good.'

The corridor was empty. The students were gone, headed home for the weekend, most of them with books under their arms. David should have been standing, waiting, but he wasn't. Julie knew it was only a reprieve. He wouldn't come all this way, then leave that easily. She felt the breath drain out of her, and drew it back in. All right. Her classroom, a load of marking for the weekend. If he came to her door at home——

This was stupid. She couldn't spend her life quivering because David might turn up. It didn't make any sense, this need to hide from him. It was only a few hours out of a lifetime. What did sex mean these days? She shivered and admitted that it meant a lot to her. Intimacy, and she had never given it lightly. Damn it, she wouldn't have thought David would either. That just showed that you didn't know people, just thought you did. She'd always operated on instinct, and her instincts had drawn her to David. He was the last person she would have expected to hurt her.

He hadn't hurt her. It was all in her head. She knew she had welcomed his loving. It was hardly his fault that she needed something he could not give. But why did she have to see him again? Couldn't he just fade out of her life?

Her telephone was unlisted, and he might not actually know her address. She had given it to Sarah when she wrote that note, but she'd asked Sarah not to say anything to David about hearing from Julie. Just sorry I ran out, and goodbye. That was all she had written in the note.

He was not standing beside her car. She knew he wouldn't be inside it. This was the city, and of course she locked her car, as David would warn her to if he could be watching. No need to lock up on Gabriola, she had thought, but that was wrong. She should have gone over there with everything locked up—her heart, her car. She should have watched her rear-view mirror, watched herself, held herself safe.

On her car, you couldn't see where the damage had been. The body shop in Nanaimo had repaired it invisibly; the only sign left would be the higher rates on next year's insurance. So much for her safe driver discount. All right, she thought, sliding in and starting the engine. And so much for keeping her heart safe. Five years of marriage to Tom hadn't left much more than vague regret on her heart. But that one visit to Gabriola last month—all her discounts lost in one stupid visit to the past.

He was not following her; of course not. She had expected him to be in the parking area, though, had surveyed the other vehicles and seen only city cars, compact and shiny, not the sort of thing you threw a few sacks of feed into.

She drove home and parked her car underground, let herself into the building with her key card and rode up in the lift to the third floor. He was not in the corridor there either, but then it would hardly be David's style to sneak into a building. He would come by the front door.

He rang her intercom an hour later. She pushed the intercom button from her apartment. 'Yes?'

'It's David. Let me in, Julie.'

'I don't have to.' He must know that he could not force her. Even if someone else let him in, she could leave him out in the corridor, outside her locked door. If he would not leave, she could call building security. They would not hesitate to throw him out.

'You can't run away from everything.'

This time, he would be on *her* territory, not the land of her childhood dreams. She made a face at the intercom, knew she was being childish. She pushed the release buzzer.

Then she closed her bedroom door.

If he wanted talk, they would talk. She would be controlled, firm, hard—the same as he was. No need for screaming, when all she had to say was . . . that she never wanted to see him again.

She opened the door to the corridor, then went back to the kitchen. He could let himself in. She did not want to open the door with him there, his eyes watching for her welcome. She got out the chopping board. Salad and steak; she would give him exactly the same thing he had cooked for her. She heard the door open, then close. She bit her lip and concentrated on turning the onion into mince, blinking at the fumes. Stupid to start with the onion.

'You shouldn't leave your door open like that.' David's voice, coming closer, disapproving. 'This isn't Gabriola. Anyone could come in.'

'People I haven't invited?' Julie glanced at him, then away. There was nothing in his face, of course, just some masked intent she could not read. 'What are you doing in the city? You don't exactly fit here.'

His lips twitched. 'Did I leave my mucking-out boots on?'

Silly of her to try to make him out as a country bumpkin. She scraped the little mound of onions into a bowl and started on the celery. 'I presume you haven't had supper? I do owe you a meal, don't I?'

He pushed his hands into his pockets. 'Do you pay all your debts?' His trousers were elegantly cut. She made herself look away, but it was too late. She would remember the way his shoulders filled out the jacket long after he was gone. The tailor had not needed any padding to get that effect of broad strength. Her body shuddered on a wave of memory. Gentle—he could be so gentle, could drive a woman beyond sanity.

She turned abruptly to the cupboards and opened a door, took out a bowl and said grimly, 'Yes, David, I always pay my debts.' Then she snapped, 'Sit at the table. You're in the way otherwise.'

He sat, but she did not fool herself that it was meekness, not with that look in his eyes. She brought another bowl out of the cupboard, then slammed them both down on the table. 'Steak?' she said rigidly. 'I presume you like yours rare?'

'Right,' he agreed, his lips twitching.

If he laughed at her, she would slam him over the head with the frying pan. She took two steaks and dropped them into the sizzling pan. Then she went back to mangling a head of lettuce for the salad.

David said quietly, 'If we're talking about the debts you owe, there's the matter of a bed.'

She swung around, the knife in her hand.

'I put you up overnight at the farm,' he reminded her.

Their eyes locked. His told her that this was serious. He was goading her, looking for a reaction, intending to close for the kill when he got it. Why? It was insane, without reason.

'A bed?' At least she had control of her voice. 'Never let it be said I don't pay my debts. I'll make reservations for you at the Holiday Inn. Or would you prefer the Sheraton?' She held his eyes. He would have to drop *his* gaze first.

He didn't. 'Are you going to attack me with that knife?'

'It's a thought.'

'I doubt you'd go that far.' It might have been amusement in his voice, but she had seen his eyes.

She made herself turn and slice into the celery. She sensed movement and said rigidly, 'Come near me and you'll find out you're wrong.'

'Even you aren't that wild.'

'Don't count on it,' she said grimly, staring at the knife in her hand.

He knew there was no threat, but she felt his decision to wait, wondering wildly what it was he had decided to do with her. Why was he here? Where did he think she could possibly fit into his life?

He said quietly, deliberately, 'Wild enough when you're in a man's arms. You might do anything then . . . but not now.'

She felt the tension snap tight in her body, the need to scream, to hit out at him. If she did that, she would be lost. He was waiting for that, ready to take control the moment she exploded. She let her breath out slowly, forced the tension to slacken. She blinked once, twice, and something in his eyes told her that he didn't know how to handle her this way. Only if she let the restlessness take hold could he get to her.

She put the lettuce down. 'Did you get your truck back OK?' She would show him that he was not the only one with icy control of his anger.

'Yes. The keys arrived in the mail, and your instructions were quite plain.' His voice was heavy with sarcasm. 'I quite enjoyed the useless trip to Vancouver. You owe me forty dollars for parking. You could have put it into long-term parking, instead of the hourly rate.'

'I was angry.' Her lips twitched.

'I would never have guessed. Where did you run to?'

'San Francisco.' She had taken her course proposal, shut herself into a shoreside motel and buried herself in work. Two weeks, and she'd been certain that by the time she returned to take up her teaching duties, he'd have no desire to come looking for her. She had been back in Vancouver almost two weeks now, had stopped looking for him on her doorstep, checking her mailbox.

'Next time, ask before you take my truck.'

'Next time,' she snapped, '*ask* before you take my body!' Her eyes locked on to his. Behind him, the telephone started to ring.

'I did,' he said grimly.

'Before,' she repeated. 'Not when you've got me so...so...' So wound up with need that *no* wasn't even in her dictionary.

He said quietly, 'At least you can concede that there will be a next time.'

Julie walked past him to the telephone, closed her hand on the receiver and said slowly, without looking at him, 'If you're asking, the answer is no. Not in a million years. Never. And don't come looking for entrance to my bed again.'

'Molly's bed,' he corrected softly. 'When you're in mine, you won't sneak away in the middle of the night. You'll stay. And if I'm in yours, you won't wake and find me gone.'

She jerked the receiver up, snapped, 'What is it?'

'Julie?' Her mother's voice, worried and quick, in her ear.

'Mom——' Now now! Not with David watching.

'Julie? What on earth's wrong? Have you got the flu? I told you not to let those kids——'

'No, Mom, I'm fine.' He was standing in the doorway to the corridor, listening and not pretending otherwise. She could not look away. 'How's the plumbing disaster?'

She listened to her mother telling her about the city crews crawling all over the neighbourhood, the nightmare of the sewer backing up all through their pretty modern suburb. David leaned back against the doorway, not going anywhere. Julie covered the receiver with her hand and snapped, 'Go check on the steak. For heaven's sake, stop watching me like that!'

'Julie? Who's there?'

'David,' she said into the receiver, immediately regretting it because he flashed a laughing look back at her, then disappeared into the kitchen.

'You didn't tell me about any David. Is that the new man upstairs? Is he nice?'

Julie snorted. 'He's a jerk.' She said it loud enough for David to hear.

His eyes were laughing when she came into the kitchen after she had hung up. He dared her softly, 'Tell me to my face that I'm a jerk.'

'Then what?' she challenged grimly, yanking the spatula from his hands.

'I'll kiss you.'

She glared at him, her jaw working with anger. 'What the hell do you think you are? When did I invite you into my life? The way I see it, you'll grab me and jerk me into your arms in macho style and whammo, I'm back in bed!' She sucked in an angry lungful of air. 'You're a chauvinist, David. It must come of watching all those cows—bulls——' She flushed and turned away, abruptly aware that she was talking herself into a mess. She tried to turn the steak, but he would not move out of her way. In the end, she shoved the spatula back into his hands and went to the salad.

He let her set the table without saying a word, sat down across from her and started eating his steak as if it were an everyday thing, as if she had not just screamed insults at him. She knew he was laughing under that silence. He had planned this from the moment he came to Vancouver—to get under her skin, make her lose her cool. She had a temper, but it was only David who had always had the ability to drive her to madness.

'Salad dressing?' she offered aggressively.

'Please.'

'French or Thousand Island?'

'French, thanks.'

She should have thrown it at him, but she passed it in silence.

The steak was overdone, slightly tough, the silence uncomfortable.

'How's Stanley?'

'Back at university after a brief attempt to become an itinerant musician.'

She concentrated on cutting the tough steak, then said, 'He thought you were having an affair with me.'

'It was none of his business, but I am involved with you.'

Her knife jerked. The steak slid to the edge of the plate. 'No, you're not. It's over.'

He took the knife out of her hand. 'If that's so, why can't you look me in the eyes?'

She did, but his eyes were giving nothing away. She did her best to make hers the same. 'Stanley is disappointed in you.'

'He was out of line and he knows it. I've talked to him.'

'And told him what? A man has his needs?'
She swallowed painfully. 'Is that what it was
about? Conquering available women? Macho
sexuality?'

'Don't be stupid!' His grip on her wrist
tightened.

'You're hurting me!'

He released her hand.

She managed to keep her voice very matter-
of-fact. 'I don't fit in your life, and you sure
as hell don't fit into mine.'

'It's too late to talk about who fits where,
Julie. You're hardly the type for a one-night
stand.'

'Aren't I?' Her voice was brittle. She got
up restlessly, took her untouched plate into
the kitchen, tossed her uncomfortable words
back at him. 'All right, so I'm not. Maybe I
just had to get you out of my...out of my
system. I had this thing about you when I was
a kid. For heaven's sake, you—you know
that.' She prowled back to the dining room
table, her hands spread out on the surface of
the table, eyes dark and angry. 'You know I
did.'

'A long time ago.' He was watching her as
if waiting for something he could use. 'You're
no child.'

'In—in a way, I never got over it. So, you see, I had to——'

'I'm to believe you went to bed with me to exorcise childish ghosts?' He shook his head. 'Don't be a fool, Julie. That was no child in my arms.'

She shivered. 'What is it you want?'

'You know what I want.'

She shook her hair back, felt it wild around her face, her neck. 'To take me to bed again?'

He smiled without humour. 'Let's call it a relationship. It sounds better that way.'

'What? Once a month? Twice? Every week?' A lump of pain was growing in her chest. 'Do I go to your place? Or will you come here? Tear yourself away from your damned cows?'

He leaned back in his chair, arms resting lightly on the table. 'Either,' he said quietly. 'Both.'

'You've got to be crazy! You and I? An affair? You're right out to lunch! Everything—— For heaven's—— We can't be together ten minutes without getting into an argument!'

He stood up, pushing the table away. She whispered, 'Don't touch me. Whatever you do, just don't touch me.'

'Afraid?' he taunted softly.

This was beyond games, battles. She said harshly, 'You're damned right I'm scared! This is a big mistake. I don't know why you haven't realised that yet. Even you can have an impulse, can't you? A...roll in the hay. It's over. Will you...please go away?'

'Is there another man?'

She stared at him, wondering if he would believe a lie. Then he moved, two steps closer. She backed up a step, but when he touched her she could not breathe. He said softly, 'In my arms, you don't feel like a woman who belongs to another man.'

She closed her eyes tightly and willed herself to move. She knew how it would be. He wanted her, but somehow he would ensure that she was the only one who lost control. She could not bear for him to look down on her when she was begging him to love her, and somehow remain separate from it.

'Are you still in love with Tom?'

She spat out, 'Now *you're* being the fool!'

He brushed her tangled hair back from her face, and she jerked back. 'Don't do that! Don't—— What do you think I am? A doll for you to use?' She saw the flush paint his cheeks—anger. She stepped back, eyeing him warily. He had always been the one in control. Even that night . . .

He said, 'You didn't push me away the night we made love.'

'No,' she agreed, and somehow even that feeling was dead in her. 'You knew I wouldn't, didn't you? You planned it, right from the kiss outside Sarah's to lure me into the woods.'

'You came.'

'You knew I wouldn't have chosen it.' She moved impatiently. 'You knew exactly what you were going to do when you came over to Sarah's that night, didn't you? After you kissed me, when Stanley—you knew I was . . . susceptible. You knew you could seduce me, didn't you? Knew you could change my mind.'

He did not answer, but there was no need. She hissed, 'When you said let's go for a walk, you meant us to end up at Molly's house. Didn't you?'

He said flatly, 'You were playing games with yourself. You're playing games now. You said it yourself, you don't make decisions. You waffle around and go with the moment.'

'So you manipulated the moment?' She should be screaming, and didn't know why she wasn't. 'You knew I wasn't comfortable about it, didn't you?'

'Of course I did. Why do you think I——'

'Manipulated me into your—into Molly's bed?' Julie closed her eyes and said wearily, 'You like having control? How important is it?'

'Control's got nothing to do with it.' But he was lying. She sensed it, knew as he turned to pace to the window that somehow she had found her mark.

She said quietly, intensely, 'I don't want to be controlled, David. I especially don't want to be controlled by a man who has no respect for me, who thinks he can run over my wishes and substitute his.'

'This isn't about control, Julie.'

She said on a note of discovery, 'Yes, it is. That's all it's about.' She closed her eyes. 'David, leave me alone.'

She heard him going, the slick sound of his jacket sliding on. She felt dead, empty; she could not believe it was that easy, that he would go. She clenched her hands in on themselves and hoped that she would not go to him, would not get in range of his tender touch, to be seduced by sensation.

When she opened her eyes, he was there, a couple of feet away, his jacket on, one hand in his pocket. He said, 'I'll pick you up tomorrow morning.' There was no friendliness in his eyes, not even desire. A deep stubbornness, perhaps. 'We'll spend the day together.'

'We'll fight.'

'Perhaps.'

'Why? What do you want from me?' She laughed bitterly. 'You don't want to marry me, do you? Do you want to turn me into Sandy? It's not possible.' She remembered that other time, child's pain. 'Maybe I thought that would be a good idea when I was thirteen, but I'm not so young now—that would be the stupidest idea I've heard in a long time.'

David's eyes were expressionless. He asked, 'Are you on the Pill?'

She swallowed dryness in her throat and shook her head.

He caught her chin with his fingers, brushed his lips against hers. She shivered, and she could see his eyes. He felt nothing. Had she killed it by dragging his wife's name into it? Or had there been nothing in the first place? She whispered, 'What do you want out of this? Why?'

'I'll pick you up at ten.' His thumb brushed across her lips. 'You won't run away this time?'

She shrugged.

'Is there any chance you could be pregnant?'

'No.'

'See a doctor next week.'

'I don't have a say in this?' She glared at him. 'What am I? Part of your damned harem?'

'Do you want to have my child?'

It hurt, holding his gaze. 'No,' she said steadily, knowing it was a lie, knowing she could not do it because that was what had happened with Sandy and she could never be Sandy.

'Then see the doctor,' he suggested. 'Because if you drive me to—it could happen, and you know damned well it's true.'

'If I drive you to what?' She should be silent, but it was wrong, didn't fit. David was the one in control, even a David driven with need and passion.

'Ten o'clock,' he said grimly.

'Why? You don't even like me.'

He stopped with his hand on the doorknob. 'Like? I don't know. I would think you'd call it an obsession.' She saw his jaw jerk and he said grimly, 'I'm not enjoying it.'

Could a woman be forced into an affair with a man? Forced, because he had control of her in ways she could not fight, held her heart in his hard, dark eyes. Could she handle an affair with him? Not likely, when she was half destroyed after one intimate night. Don't run, he had said. She was not sure she could, or if she wanted to.

CHAPTER SEVEN

'This is a bad idea,' Julie said abruptly, staring through the windscreen at Vancouver's first September rainstorm.

David shifted gears on his rental car. 'Next left?'

'Yes. No, I don't think we should——' She glanced at him and surprised a half-smile on his lips. He thought this was funny? He would change his mind when her mother and father started the grand inquisition. The first man she had brought home in years! She stared at a dingy green car on the other side of the intersection as David pulled to a stop in the turning lane. 'My mother——'

'Your mother what?'

Julie shifted uncomfortably. 'She's always...'

'She wants you to get married again.'

She turned to stare out of her window at a woman pushing a baby buggy through the rain. 'I suppose that's natural, but—— Well,

I never take my dates out here. It's embarrassing.'

'I'll survive it.'

It had been a stupid idea, born of anger at his assumption that she would spend the day with him, her inability to say no. He had rung her buzzer from downstairs promptly at ten that morning. She had gone down, greeting him at the front door, not meeting his eyes, had said briskly, 'I don't know what you'd planned, but I've promised my mother I'd come over today. So if you want to tag along, you're welcome, but...'

She had expected him to protest. A man who wanted an affair didn't want to visit his—his lover's mother. What had she thought to gain? Making trouble, she decided miserably. Somehow David always roused that urge in her; but she was not going to change David's determination to possess her by throwing in her mother. She stared at David's hands on the wheel, his long fingers confident in the city traffic. She had expected the pick-up truck from the farm, not a quiet, sleek rental car.

She curled her own fingers tightly into her hands. David's lover. She had lain awake all night, knowing it would never be enough, yet almost certain she could not find the strength to draw back from this frighteningly inevitable relationship.

David stopped the car outside a sprawling suburban home with a two-car garage. 'Is this it?'

'Oh, brother!' Julie breathed. 'Wally's here!' He was standing at the doorway, looking this way. She pressed back against the seat and muttered, 'Let's just turn around and go.'

David's lips twitched. 'In my wildest dreams, I wouldn't imagine you afraid of Wally.'

'It isn't Wally so much as—all of them together.'

They would be asking questions, open curiosity in their eyes. Some of the questions would be silent, reserved for later. Tomorrow, over Sunday dinner. Next week, on the telephone. Her mother would bring David's name into questions and speculations for weeks and months to come.

David's hand found hers on the seat and closed over it. 'It won't be that bad. Come on.'

She opened the door and slid out. David was right behind her, but she did not look back. She could hear it now. Did you see how she looked at him?... Remember how she used to tag after him all the time?... Julie and David? But they were always arguing, weren't they?... What would he see in her?... It won't last, Julie. Find someone else... Remember his wife? They were the perfect couple. He's still in love with her, always in love with her. He'll never put you in her place... her place, not yours.

Wally was staring past her, at David. Julie stopped in front of him. 'Hi, Wally. This is——'

'David McNaughton,' said Wally in a cold voice.

David reached past her with a hand that Wally automatically shook. David's other arm curled around Julie, hand resting possessively on her hip. 'It's been a while since I've seen you on Gabriola, Wally.'

Julie shifted slightly, and tried to move away, but David only drew her closer.

Her brother said, 'So how's Gabriola? And your family?'

Julie said, 'Pat's married. You remember Pat McNaughton?'

'And Sarah,' added David. 'Happily married.'

There was an antagonism between the two men that Julie could not quite understand. Wally was—what? Six years younger than David. She would have thought they would hardly remember each other.

David was saying, 'Julie tells me you're in real estate now.'

With Wally talking about real estate trends, Julie knew it was a good time to slip away and go inside to greet her mother without David's arm holding her close. She moved to step away, but his grip tightened imperceptibly. He glanced down at her, eyes telling her plainly that he was not going to free her.

Unless she made a scene. She thought that he was not quite sure she wouldn't.

They went inside together, Julie in the curve of David's arm. Her mother was just coming down the corridor, her eyes widening at the sight of her daughter entangled with a man. Julie tried to move away.

David said in a low voice, 'Give it up.'

'I'll kill you for this!' she hissed.

He murmured back, 'I'll look forward to the battle,' as if he *enjoyed* fighting with her.

'Hi, Mom,' she said weakly.

'Hello, Mrs Charters.' David was smiling. 'It's David McNaughton, from Gabriola. It's nice to see you again.'

'David Mc——but aren't you——? Hello, David.'

They ended up around the kitchen table, her mother serving tea and questions. Luckily, her father wasn't there to ask about David's prospects and what his intentions were. Julie knew she had lost control of the day. She watched David warily, suspicious because his eyes were so carefully blank. It was not like him to make mischief—at least, she had never thought it was.

'Where's Dad?' she asked uneasily.

'Down at the golf course,' said her mother.

Julie's eyes widened. 'Playing golf in the rain?'

Her mother laughed, smiling at David. 'They're planning the new course—a meeting of the executive. You'll stay for lunch, won't you, David?'

'No,' said Julie abruptly. 'We've got reservations at——'

'We can change our plans,' David said easily, reaching across to cover her hand with his. 'We'd love to, Mrs Charters.'

'Call me Sandra,' invited her mother. Julie jerked her hand away as her mother shifted into organiser mode. 'Now, Wally, why don't you show David the new recreation-room downstairs? He might have some ideas for that end wall. And Julie, you can come help me with lunch.'

Julie followed her mother into the kitchen, knowing this was one scene she could not avoid.

Her mother demanded, 'Last night, on the phone, you said *David*?'

She had forgotten that; she would never have mentioned a man's name to her mother, except in a moment of madness. Her mother picked up a loaf of bread and demanded softly, 'You said he was a jerk. David McNaughton?'

'It was a joke.'

'What kind of a joke is that? What were you and he——?'

'We were *fighting*. Arguing. He's always been so darned...bossy. And there's nothing between us, nothing at all, so don't, for goodness' sake, start asking questions about us or——'

Her mother placed both hands on the kitchen table and fixed the Spanish

Inquisition look on Julie. 'He had his arms around you, and I saw you whispering to him. So what's going on?'

Julie knew the answer. Madness, David and Julie and disaster somewhere not too far into the future.

Her mother said, 'He's a farmer, isn't he? He'd never move to the city.'

'What makes you so sure I wouldn't move out there?' David was offering weekends, and she had to start fantasising a lifetime! Fool!

'To a little island? You mean——'

'I don't mean anything!' Julie's voice rose in frustration. 'Mother, there's nothing. Don't make something of it. He was just...just in town and——'

'He's married,' her mother said flatly. 'I'd forgotten. It's so long since we spent summers over there. But I remember now—he married that girl he met at university. Skinny girl, long blonde hair. They had a baby—— Julie, I know you're a modern woman, divorced and all, but—— A married man!'

'He's widowed,' Julie gritted out. 'And we're *not*——'

'Widowed?' Her mother relaxed, laying out pieces of fresh bread on the cutting block. 'What do you think, Julie? Egg salad? Or the ham? Or I could lay out a selection. How long ago did his wife die? Do you think he likes ham?'

'Mom, just make whatever's easiest.' Julie turned away to get the butter out of the fridge.

'How long since the wife died?'

Julie slapped butter on to a piece of bread. 'Three years.'

'Well, that's long enough. What about the baby? Or did they have more?'

Julie banged the knife down, closed her eyes and said tightly, 'The baby's eighteen and off at university. There aren't any other children. Will you *stop* this?'

Her mother took the knife out from under Julie's fingers. 'Don't get in a state, dear, I'm just concerned about you. You're my daughter, and it's not natural for a woman your age to live alone.'

She reached for the knife back, but her mother was efficiently buttering bread. She said weakly, 'That's nonsense—about it not being natural, I mean.'

'Cut the ham, dear. You're quite good at that. And it's not nonsense. You'd have a much better temper if you were married.'

Hopeless. It was hopeless. What insanity had driven her to bring David *here* of all places? Marriage was the last thing David was looking for, but she could hardly tell her mother that.

She said grimly, 'Haven't you read any of the recent studies on single women? Women do quite well living alone, have lower stress levels than married women.'

Her mother mused, 'He must be quite well off, wouldn't you think? As I remember, the McNaughtons owned a good bit of that island. That subdivision on top of the hill was all McNaughton land. And don't they own property somewhere else? Fiji? Bermuda? Somewhere like that.'

Julie tried changing the subject. 'What about this new golf course? What are they planning?'

'Who knows, dear? Golf is your father's affair.' Her mother touched immaculate grey hair. 'I just like to see him get out and have an interest. Do you think David likes apple pie?'

'Your apple pie? He'd be crazy if he didn't.'

Julie's mother served David with an extra helping of pie after dinner, telling him that a big man needed to be well fed, talking as if David must be starving, living alone. Julie cringed, but David gave no sign that he was either embarrassed or annoyed.

Her mother suggested, 'You should get Julie to cook you some good meals while you're visiting Vancouver.'

'Yes,' David agreed, his eyes laughing. 'She gave me steak last night.'

'Good.' Her mother beamed. 'Would you like coffee or tea, David?'

'Tea, please.'

While her mother was preparing the tea, David said idly to Wally, 'I see a real estate sign on Julie's cottage. Your company?'

Wally agreed, 'That's right. Julie decided to list it.'

'What kind of market do you see?'

Her brother shrugged. 'I'm sure I can find someone to take it. Gulf Islands properties have a steady demand.'

'Not nearly what they'll have if the bridge is announced,' suggested David quietly.

Angry amusement in David's eyes, wariness in Wally's.

Julie demanded, 'What bridge? What are you talking about, David?'

'Julie's not up on Gabriola issues,' he said, holding Wally's eyes. 'But *you* are, aren't you? Why didn't you advise Julie to hang on to that property? If that bridge is announced, she could sell it for double without even trying.'

Wally shifted in his seat, called out casually, 'Mom? How's that coffee coming?'

'Tea, Wally.' His mother's voice was muffled, coming from the kitchen. 'David wants tea. It'll be ready in two minutes.'

Julie stared at Wally. She should have known there was something! 'You knew about the bridge?'

Wally muttered, 'It must be a local issue.' He shifted uneasily in his chair. 'David would be more up on it than I. If he's right about the short link bridge—well...' he spread his hands '...it might be better to keep the place off the market for a while.'

'Short link?' It rang a bell in Julie's memory.

News items, demonstrations and controversy. One faction wanted to shorten the Vancouver to Vancouver Island ferry route with a bridge on to some of the gulf islands. Another feared a bridge would destroy the special quality of island life.

'The short link involves Gabriola?'

David nodded. 'From Vancouver Island to Mudge Island, then across False Narrows to Gabriola.'

'A bridge to Gabriola? You wouldn't want that, would you?' He had always lived on Gabriola, life surrounded by the water was a part of him.

He said, 'I'm not sure Gabriolans will have that much say. It's a transportation issue, involving all Vancouver Island. If there's a bridge, then a highway across Gabriola to the new, proposed ferry site would run——'

'Enough business.' Wally stood up abruptly. 'I get tired of talking real estate on my time off. What have you been doing in that school of yours, Julie? Sharon and I——'

Julie said brusquely, 'I'm going to take the property off the market.'

Next week she would find out just what was involved in this bridge thing. She didn't suppose there was much she could do, but she could write some letters to members of the Legislative Assembly, at least. She remembered seeing a drawing on the front page of a newspaper, not looking because what did a bridge matter to her? She'd call Ann at the library tomorrow, see if she couldn't dig out that old newspaper. Her property would be right in the line of that proposed highway. Wally must know that or he wouldn't have hounded her so to get it on the market. He was making a fair job of dissembling now, but he had known from the beginning. If she had sold, would she have found later that Wally had an interest in the company that bought her property?

'Thanks for exposing Wally's devious motives,' Julie said uneasily as David drove away from her parents' house.

He glanced at her. 'I've never trusted your brother particularly.'

She toyed with the strap of her bag. 'You two had some sort of a run-in?'

'Hm.'

She snapped, 'You can be a real stone-face when you try, you know.' She saw his lips twitch, and she asked, 'What was it about?'

He glanced at her, then back at the traffic light ahead. 'I warned him off Sarah. They'd been seeing each other, and I'd heard some things—— I figured he was up to no good with her.'

'No wonder he was glaring at you. He'd have hated that.'

He nodded. 'I know. And I imagine Sarah might have looked after herself all right. I was something of an arrogant older brother.'

'Protective.' She smiled and twisted her fingers together. 'I believe that. Do you see me as your younger sister? Looking out for my interests?'

'No.'

She didn't believe him, not completely. He had always interfered in her affairs. He always would, as long as...until it was over. But today could be a first, because David had interfered in her affairs and she had thanked him.

He looked quietly relaxed, as if he had enjoyed himself. She mused, 'Do you know, we might have made history. We've just spent four hours without fighting?'

He chuckled. 'Minor skirmishes. I don't give us the rest of the day before we have a major battle.'

She studied the hard lines of his face, and saw a man who would not have to raise his voice to win. 'David, do you fight with other people?' He had defeated Wally with a few words.

He said wryly, 'Only you.'

That wasn't exactly a compliment. 'What is it you want to do?' she asked abruptly, staring at the blue spot between two angry clouds.

'A walk through Stanley Park. Dinner at the Bayshore afterwards.'

'I'm not dressed for the Bayshore.' She hugged herself. 'Neither are you—too casual.' She thought he would get in with no trouble. Casual, but potently attractive in his dark trousers and that soft cashmere sweater.

'We can change.'

She swallowed. 'And afterwards? What then?'

David braked to a stop for a red light. She decided that the blue spot in the sky might turn into something brighter. He touched her hair with his hand, finger-combing the wild curls. 'What then?' he mused, his eyes flaring. 'What do you want it to be?'

She hugged her arms tighter, trying not to succumb to the trembling sensations from his fingers in her hair. 'Dancing?' she suggested uneasily.

'OK.'

'Then what?' His arms around her. Soft music. Her voice cracked. 'To bed? Is that what you've planned?'

'If you want,' he agreed quietly.

'Damn you!' she whispered harshly. 'You're doing this deliberately, aren't you? If *I* want? What are you doing here? Yesterday you said once wasn't enough. Now I'm asking what this is supposed to—how you see this...this *affair* being—being carried on, and you're saying "yes" and "OK" and "if you want!" You don't mean a damned word of it! I know you don't!'

He caught her hair and cupped her head with his strong fingers, turning her head to face him. The fool inside Julie ached for his lips to close on hers.

He said harshly, 'Starting a fight won't make the issue go away.'

She gulped. 'You—— All right, then. I——' She clenched her jaw and made herself say, 'I don't want to go to bed with you.'

'Lying won't help either.'

'Damn you!' She felt the muscles of her neck cording up. 'Let go of me!'

Behind them, a horn blared impatiently.

'The light's green,' she whispered.

David released her and turned back to the wheel, his lips pressed tightly together. She could feel the anger in him—controlled fury, always controlled.

They were somewhere on Kingsway Street, surrounded by traffic. 'Where are you taking me?' she demanded.

No answer.

'David, I don't want to go to bed with you. I don't!'

He signalled for a turn, then slipped through a break in the traffic on to a side-street. 'You're lying,' he said evenly, 'but don't worry about it. We'll wait.'

She gasped, closed her eyelids tightly and gritted out, 'Do you know how damned arrogant that sounds?'

Abruptly, he pulled into a parking space along the side of the road. He turned towards her, his arm behind her, fingers threading through her free curls. His tension gone, his face quietly determined. He said, 'I know what happens when we're together, when I touch you.'

She shook her head mutely. He slid his fingers deeper into her hair, cradled her head as he bent to touch his lips to her. He touched her face, pressed his lips to her eyelids with agonising gentleness, 'Even when you hold back, I can feel your response. Your eyes, so deep, a man could drown there. Your lips...your breasts, swelling...hardening.'

He brushed his thumb across the hard peak of one.

She bit down hard to stop the gasp of desire, clenched her hands in on themselves and whispered slowly, 'You're a bastard, David. Why would I want to have an affair with anyone so bloody arrogant?'

His thumb traced the rigid edge of her jaw. His finger slipped up to her lips, parting them and slipping between. He murmured, 'Stop calling it an affair, Julie. It's a relationship.'

She turned her head to stare into his eyes. 'What's the difference?'

If he answered, it was only in his eyes. His thumb brushed across her lips. She wanted him to kiss her, needed his mouth against hers. She managed somehow to close her lips tightly against the soft caress of his thumb. The sensation moved to her cheek, and she jerked her head away.

'If we go out . . . dinner and dancing and—— I want to go home alone after, to—to bed alone.'

He said huskily, 'Come to Gabriola next weekend.' His thumb slipped to her throat, sensual pressure on her flesh.

She closed her eyes. How long? How many weekends? How many weekdays waiting for David? Aching.

'You can get the six o'clock ferry. I'll pick you up on the Nanaimo side.'

'I have a weekend practice with the drama club next Saturday.' She wished her voice did not sound so strained, so unnatural. His touch hardened, thumb pressing in under the point of her jaw.

'Would you lie to me?'

She shivered. 'I—I don't think so.'

'I'd know if you did.'

'I know you would.' She shuddered. There was nothing she could hide from him. That was what frightened her so.

'I'll come here next weekend. Can you come to me the weekend after?'

She rolled her head away from his touch, stared at a street of houses crowded together outside her car. 'David, you didn't answer me. I said I want to go home alone tonight, to bed alone.'

'I won't take anything you're not offering me, Julie.' His fingers tangled in her curls.

She muttered angrily, 'That's no damned assurance at all!'

He brought her face back so that he could see her eyes. 'Can't you hear what you're saying? You want me as much as I want you.'

More, she thought miserably. More than he ever would. She would be the slave of her own needs, would be driven to fight him everywhere...except on the one battleground where she could not win.

'Why fight it, Julie?'

'Self-preservation,' she whispered with painful honesty. 'We'll just mess each other up. We're crazy to try it.'

His fingers caught her hair and threaded through again. She fought the urge to close her eyes and melt into him. When he touched her hair, she could feel the caress right through to her heart.

He murmured, 'Since when were you afraid to take a chance?'

'Always,' she answered seriously. 'You just never understood.'

'Then help me understand.' His eyes held hers and she shook her head mutely. 'Will you come the weekend after next?'

'Where...where do you want me to stay?'

'At the farm. With me.'

In his bed? It would come to that, of course. Was it the same bed he and Sandy had loved in? She shuddered and whispered, 'What will your family think?'

'That I have a woman staying the weekend.'

'Do you——? I've got marking to do, I can't just take a whole weekend off. There'll be the first drafts of the plays from my drama class.'

'Bring them.'

'You don't take no for an answer, do you?'

'No.' The smile was in his eyes.

Julie's lips twitched. 'I'm supposed to go off for a...for a weekend with a man and take marking along to do in his living-room?'

'A weekend with *me*,' he corrected. 'And you can use my office if you don't like the living-room.' The laughter left his eyes and they were black. 'What did you bring to your other men? The weekend woman? Not the teacher?' Her lips parted without words. He said, 'I want it all. Don't leave part of yourself behind.'

It was worse than she had thought. He would drain her, leave her with nothing in her life that was free of him. She whispered, 'I've never done it before. Gone off for a weekend with a...with a...'

'A lover?'

She wished she could look away from him, but it was hopeless. She said, 'The closest was when I ran away with Tom.' She had been seventeen then, which was some kind of excuse. But now, fourteen years later, she should have more sense than to jump off the edge of the universe for a man.

David possessed her chin in his palm, pinning her eyes with his. 'I won't hurt you, Julie.'

She stared back at him. He would not mean to hurt her, of course, but it would happen. The end would come. Impossible match, Julie and David. Opposites, two individuals who could not share the same space without waging war. Or making love, but she was not sure you could call it love, not the way it had been in Molly McNaughton's empty cabin— David holding back, herself beyond all boundaries. It would not happen again like that. She would stop it somehow, keep some part of herself separate, hidden away from him.

'All right,' she said finally. 'But I want you to promise one thing. If I say no——'

'Don't touch?' he asked softly. He traced her lips with his finger, followed the curve of her throat down to the V of her blouse. 'I don't think I can do that. Not if your body reaches for me, while your lips tell lies.'

She shook her head and whispered, 'It wasn't like that.'

'Wasn't it?'

She ached for him to kiss her, for his lips to come down and bury themselves in her mouth. She needed to melt against him, to pull him close with her arms, to thread her fingers through his hair, the sinews of his shoulders and his arms. His body tight against hers, hardness driven into her softness.

He said, 'There's more between us than the words. I can read your signals as if they were my own. If you send a no, I'm not going to push past it—but be honest with yourself. There haven't been any refusals around. Even now, I can feel——'

'Don't say it.' She turned her face into his shoulder, feeling his hardness twisted against her. She admitted shakily, 'I'm scared. You won't understand that, but I'm terrified.'

His hands slid across her back. 'Just let it happen. Stop fighting me so.'

It was a strange day. The tension was always there, just beneath the surface. They went to Stanley Park. Not to the quiet, lonely paths where he could have taken her in his arms and turned her resistance to nonsense. Instead, David took her among other people. To the aquarium at the park, where they watched the whales performing with the dolphins. To the sea wall, where they walked with linked hands while he asked her about Unlimited Potential and her dream of some day having a school of her own.

'I've got my Masters degree,' she told him, 'but I think my chances would be better if I went on and got my doctorate.' She had never seriously intended to go back to university again, but she decided now, with David's hand enclosing hers and the sun warring with black clouds overhead, that it was the only thing to do. Plans, she thought wildly. It was good to keep her mind on plans for her future, to keep this thing where it belonged. Short range—that was all there would ever be for herself and David.

'Where exactly would that get you? Would it make you a better teacher?'

She shrugged. 'It would give me more credibility, a better chance of getting into administration.'

'Stay with the kids, Julie. You've got magic for them.' He looked out over the harbour, to the building-covered hills on the other side.

'Don't hide that away in an office, telling other teachers how to do something they can never do as well as you.'

'You think I'd be no good in administration?' She frowned. 'Don't be so sure. I could surprise you.'

'You'll always surprise me.'

She sighed in confusion, but he turned the conversation away from the edge of an argument, leading her up a grassy hill to where he pointed out a squirrel running along a big overhead branch. When he turned to look at her, his eyes were filled with all the things that were held back. The promise of what would happen between them, the inevitable joining. They both knew she would be his if he reached, but he held back.

He took her to the promised dinner at the Bayshore, elegance and quiet tastefulness. When they danced afterwards, David's arms encircled her. It took the cool night air, the slow drive home, to bring sanity back to Julie after that slow, shattering time in his arms. But at the end of the evening, when she had her lips parted to protest his advances, her flesh trembling with anticipation, he left her at the entrance to her building without even a goodnight kiss.

He stared at her with shuttered eyes and said quietly, 'Goodnight, Julie. I'll pick you up at the same time tomorrow.'

She tried to keep the confusion out of her eyes, said warningly, 'I have marking to do.'

'All right, Bring it with you.'

Sunday. It began as an incredibly wonderful day—simple pleasures. Sitting on the grass in the park on a blanket she had brought, snacking from a picnic basket she'd made, laughing as David slipped olives into her mouth while her hands were full with marking pen and paper. Reading over her students' versions of what they wanted to do with their lives. David reading the ones she had marked, asking questions about what she really wanted to get when she gave an assignment like that.

'Just to know them,' she said absently, circling a word on the page in front of her. She was sprawled on her stomach, chin propped on her elbows, papers anchored against the breeze by an empty jar. 'They're a new class. I try to get them to loosen up, to reveal something about themselves so I know how I can get to them.'

'You're good at that, aren't you?'

She twisted to look up at him, startled by the strange note in his voice. A moment ago his eyes had been warm and amused, but he had his mask on now, his eyes flat and dark. He said almost angrily, 'Poking and prodding and knowing instinctively how to get a reaction.'

'Are we talking about my students?' She swallowed a dry lump in her throat.

'You know damned well we're not.' He bent over and took her mouth in a kiss that had nothing of gentleness in it. When he pulled away, her lips felt swollen and bruised.

She touched her lower lip with her tongue, asked in a whisper, 'Why are you angry?' So often, she seemed unable to stop digging at him, trying to get a reaction from him. But this time——

'It's not aimless at all, is it?' His voice was soft, empty of emotion, but something dangerous was lying behind his eyes.

'What's not aimless?'

'You. I always thought you were running from one thing to the next, jumping from disaster to disaster like a fool, but I had it wrong.'

'I don't understand what you're saying.' She wished she could look away.

'You've got a good instinct for self-preservation.' His voice made it sound an insult, not a compliment. 'It all looks like impulse, but you manipulate us all, just like those students. You've got an instinct for our weaknesses. I thought Tom took advantage of you, but it was the other way around, wasn't it?'

She sat up abruptly, her hands tightening together in her lap, the folds of her cotton skirt strewn around her on the blanket.

He grated out, 'You wanted a man, a husband. You didn't want anyone that would get at you too deeply, just someone to be there when you needed him, to go away when you didn't. That's why you fight me, isn't it? Because I won't go away when you want.'

'Tom left me.' She could feel pain welling up in her throat. 'What do you think I am, a monster? Do you think I wanted him to go? Used him and——'

'I think you drove him away by holding yourself separate from him. A man needs warmth, loving. You look like a woman who's all warmth and passion, but you seal it off, don't you? Tom didn't get it, did he?'

She scrambled up to her feet, her breath coming in painful gulps. 'What is this? I

didn't ask you to be here with me! I'm not
the one who wanted a relationship.'

He was on his feet suddenly. They were
inches apart, facing each other like two
fighters waiting for the bell. Abruptly, he
reached for her shoulders and pulled her
roughly to him. 'You don't like that, do you,
Julie? Needing me . . .' He smoothed her body
along the length of his with impatient hands
on her back. She fought the sensations that
swept her, but he knew what his touch did.

'Stop it,' she whispered, but his body was
hard with more than desire.

He said, 'You picked Tom for your first
lover because you could control him, could
control the situation.' He bent and sought her
lips with his, forced his kiss against her rigid
mouth, then gentled to brush her lips with
tender passion.

He pulled back in the instant when she lost
the battle and melted against him. He said
harshly, 'With me you're out of control and
you hate it. So you keep needling, trying to
make me lose my cool, driving me mad.'

'No,' she whispered, but his eyes told her
he knew better. His hands slipped into her
hair, cradled her head and drew her back with
a tenderness she could not fight.

'You'd rather I left, wouldn't you?' he demanded roughly. 'Rather be alone, cold and lonely, than take a chance on losing control.'

She licked her lips, felt his eyes on the motion. She said miserably, 'You're the one who won't lose control. When you made love to me I felt as if you'd used me, as if in a very real . . . as if you'd stripped me of every scrap of covering, left me naked and yourself fully clothed.'

Abruptly, she was free.

She hugged herself, staring at his harsh face, the deep lines beside his mouth, the shuttered eyes. 'It's true,' she whispered. 'You want me at your mercy. What will you do with me, David, when I'm exposed and vulnerable, and you're still all sealed inside yourself? Will you destroy me?'

'Don't be a damned fool,' he said harshly.

She stepped back, putting dead air between them. 'Take me home. I want to go home.'

'None too soon,' he muttered grimly. 'It's either that, or I start throttling you.'

She thought he would not come the next week. She thought she had finally driven him away, but he was there on Friday, standing in the doorway of her last class, watching.

She felt a painful stab of joy. And fear, knowing she could not turn away. Knowing that, eventually, he would leave her alone.

CHAPTER EIGHT

JULIE brought her students' *Hamlet* assignments with her the weekend she went to visit David at Gabriola. She did not understand why he wanted her after the disaster of last weekend, but he called on Thursday night, his voice brisk and impersonal.

'Julie, why don't you catch the bus from downtown Vancouver? I can pick you up at the terminal in Nanaimo, save you all that driving.'

Leave her at his mercy, stranded on Gabriola without a car? 'No,' she said, panicked. 'I'll bring my own car.'

She wondered if she would have gone if she hadn't heard from him. He might call it a relationship, but it was war more often than peace. Last weekend he had taken her to dinner from the school, then back to her apartment. He had spent the evening prowling through her records and books—restless, unlike the David she thought she knew.

They had not touched once the whole weekend. Not one kiss. Not even the familiar caress of his fingers in her hair. Julie had tried to keep space between them, to avoid accidental contact. It had not been difficult. David had seemed equally eager to avoid touching. They had not argued, not even the smallest skirmish, but it might have been better if they had. Her nerves had been screaming by the time he left on Sunday evening. The explosion was there, waiting.

On Friday afternoon she left straight from school, drove across Lion's Gate Bridge with a million other weekenders, then crawled out to Horseshoe Bay in an endless snarl of traffic. At the toll booth, she was given a one-sailing delay for the ferry to Nanaimo. She watched the ferry come in and load without her, knowing she would have been on it if she'd taken the bus. As it was, it would be dark by the time she got to Gabriola.

Two hours more, sitting in the ferry line-up, worrying about David, the look in his eyes each time he greeted her. She wanted it to be love, wondered what it really was. She took out her marking, but fifteen versions of how Shakespeare should have done *Hamlet* seemed an impossible chore sitting in her car. She would take them upstairs on the ferry—yes, that was the way to do it. She would get a table in the cafeteria and do some of her marking then, arrive at David's with the marking all done, free for the weekend.

She went for a restless walk, but her watch had stopped and she was afraid to get too far from her car. The day had a feeling of disaster in it. The ferry might come while she was off at the other end of the terminal. She'd miss her sailing, all the other cars driving around her empty Suzuki. She would run back and . . . be too late.

Two hours seemed forever, but finally the ship docked and the cars began to board. The ferry, of course, was packed. Julie flooded up from the car deck in a crowd of people, found herself in a ridiculous line-up for the cafeteria. She had not eaten supper, but she would never get to the head of this queue. She gave up her place and went looking for somewhere to sit quietly. All the lounges were packed with people. The whole world was journeying to Vancouver Island for the weekend.

She stopped at a telephone booth tucked in a corner. Should she call David? He would have expected her earlier. Right after school, he had said, but it was already past seven. She went up to the telephone, but, although it looked like a regular telephone, it must be some kind of radio phone, and she was uncertain how to use it. She went outside to let the wind blow through her hair, fresh air for her confused mind. Then she had to dash into the ladies' room and try to untangle the mass of her curls before the ferry docked.

In Nanaimo, she drove to the Gabriola ferry, getting there just in time to see the *Quinsam* leaving.

'It'll be an hour,' said the cheerful clerk in the little toll building. 'We're behind schedule—had an ambulance run this afternoon. Do you want one ticket or a commuter book?'

Julie's heart skipped a beat. 'An ambulance? Who?' But the clerk wasn't sure who had been in the ambulance. Julie asked, 'What does a book of tickets cost?'

It was quite a saving over the single rate for a car and driver, but buying it was making the assumption that . . . that this was going to last long enough to use the tickets. She didn't even know why she was here, because one more night in David's arms would destroy her.

'Yes,' she said, 'I'll take a book.' *Fool*, her heart whispered.

It could not be David who had ridden the ambulance. Somehow she was certain she would have known if it were David.

She went into the building while she waited, threaded through Gabriolans who were strangers to her, read notices on the bulletin board much like those she remembered from the summers she and Tom had used the cottage. Pigs for sale, will slaughter...five loads of fill, good topsoil, will deliver...student needs ride to college from 8 a.m. ferry...wanted, three-bedroom house for long-time Gabriola resident.

She had a three-bedroom summer home lying empty. Her earlier decision to put it on the market had been blown wide open with David's exposure of Wally's motives. One day she might ask Wally just what he'd intended, or maybe it didn't matter. Until her return from that August visit to Gabriola, she had never seriously intended to let Wally sell the place for her; she had always known she could not trust Wally where money was involved.

She watched the ferry coming, brilliant lights in the darkness. Gabriola was only a dark shadow outside Nanaimo harbour. Was David waiting for her? Wondering when she would come? If she would come?

She felt like a magnet drawn towards north. The ferry ride was unreal. She got out of her car and walked through the passenger lounges, listening to the laughter of teenagers coming back from some sports event in Nanaimo, passing two young lovers with hands and arms entangled.

More bulletin boards. She read every notice on every board. Four lounges. Four boards. Yoga classes. New Montessori school. She could teach in a Montessori school. It would be exciting, a change, to work with younger children. An entertainer coming to the Thrasher Pub. Notices for Sarah's and Edward's bed and breakfast on McNaughton Road.

Nothing that had to do with David himself. Of course, there was no reason why there should be. She had no idea why she was looking. She turned back and closed herself in her car, staring at the lights of the Gabriola ferry landing looming near. It was dark; it was late. The farm might be empty, David gone out somewhere.

She drove too fast, tearing along North Road, needing to see him, to know he had waited for her.

His truck was there, the small pick-up parked by the farmhouse, the big dump truck further down the hill by the barn. Julie parked behind the pick-up, pushed on the hand-brake and turned off the engine. Silence, emptiness. The house was dark. She got out, watching down the hill for some sign of him in the moonlight.

'Julie?'

She swung around. He was there, in the shadows on the veranda. She went to the bottom of the stairs, said nervously, 'I got held up at Horseshoe Bay.'

'I thought you would.' His shadow loomed over her. 'Did you bring a case?'

She nodded. 'In the boot. I—the Gabriola ferry was late too. They said there was an ambulance run. It wasn't Sarah's kids? Or——'

'No. It didn't sound a siren, so it might not even have been an emergency, just someone who needed transport to hospital for more ordinary reasons.'

'I got commuter tickets.' She bit her lip, holding back the question she couldn't possibly ask. How long, David? How many books of commuter tickets will we last?

He asked, 'Have you got the key to your boot?'

She held her keys out to him. It was going to be difficult, all weekend with this stiffness between them.

He went around to the back of her little car and opened it. 'You just missed my parents. They must have left on the ferry you came on, heading down to Victoria for the weekend.'

'Thank goodness for that!' He lifted his head and she wondered what he could see, staring at her in the moonlight. She stumbled over her words. 'Wouldn't it be awkward? Are they...do they live at the farmhouse too? And—and what would I say? Hi, I'm your son's—your son's...'

'When you figure out just what you are to me, let me know,' he said quietly.

Everything, she thought. It would be so much easier if he meant less.

She should have worn a warm jacket over her light sweater. She hadn't changed after school and was still wearing the pleated rust-coloured skirt with a light green and brown sweater over it. She hugged the sweater to herself and knew the instant when David's eyes took in the curve of her breasts.

She went into the house ahead of him, finding the light switch inside the door. Had he been out here on the veranda since dark, waiting for her? Or just enjoying the quiet night and the smell of autumn on the air? She turned back to see his face in the light, but there was nothing in his expression to answer her question.

'Where do you want your case?'

Julie stared back at him, her throat dry.

'The guest-room,' he decided drily.

She followed him there, watched as he walked across the room and pulled the curtains closed. The bed was freshly made, and she thought he had meant to put her there from the first.

'Have you eaten?'

She shook her head.

'Why don't we go out, then?'

'Isn't it too late?'

David shook his head. 'Friday night. Still tourist season.'

He took her up to Sarah's, where they were treated like guests in the dining room, served with menus and charming courtesy. Little Sally laughed when she brought their salad, whispering, 'Uncle David, will you give me a tip if I serve you nicely?'

'It's a promise,' he told her, his lips twitching with humour.

Then Jeremy came, slipping in without his mother's knowledge and asking David if he could come and feed the chickens the next day.

'No more peanut butter sandwiches?' David's voice was stern, belying the warmth in his eyes. Julie tried not to watch him, but found herself unable to look away. Children penetrated his harsh exterior so easily.

'Promise,' vowed Jeremy. 'Just what you say they get, their water and grain, and can I learn to milk a cow?'

'I don't have any milk cows. Would a goat satisfy you? I could ask Mr Weston and he might let you learn to milk his goats.'

Afterwards, David and Julie went into the back, where Sally and Jeremy were insisting that their father should read them a dinosaur book.

'You guys can read them yourself,' complained Edward. 'Or wait for Molly—she's better at it.'

'Try Julie,' suggested David, and she found herself sitting in the big sofa with the serious Jeremy on one side, wide-eyed Sally on the other.

The stories were fun. Julie got the children to take parts—Jeremy acting as the big brontosaurus Bronty, Sally as the pterodactyl Terry. She tried not to be aware of David in the big easy-chair opposite, talking with Edward in a low voice, watching Julie every moment.

'I want Julie to tuck me in,' demanded Sally.

David said softly, 'And she's a girl who gets what she wants.'

'Let's go, then,' said Julie, taking Sally's hand, walking away from David. Feeling his eyes on her back.

Sarah came into Sally's bedroom just as Julie was leaving, and warned, 'Don't let my charmer talk you into another story.'

Julie grinned. 'Next time, I said.'

'And when is next time?' demanded Sarah.

Julie shrugged, avoiding her friend's eyes.

'I never imagined you and David together.'

'No, I—— Don't jump to any conclusions, Sarah.'

Sarah smoothed her hands along her trousers. 'You two always fought.'

Julie laughed uncomfortably and admitted, 'Nothing's changed.'

'Well . . .' Sarah half smiled. 'I know he can be maddening, always so certain of what he's doing. Usually right too, darn him!'

'Yes, well, that hasn't changed either.' Julie moved away towards the stairs, uncomfortable with Sarah's determination to talk about David.

Sarah said slowly, 'He dominated Sandy.'

'I'm not Sandy.' Julie felt the bands tightening around her chest.

'Not in a million years,' agreed Sarah. 'She was good at everything, better than me—a better cook, a better mother. She had no weaknesses.'

'That's crazy!' Julie wished Sarah would stop. She didn't need telling how wonderful Sandy McNaughton had been. David had told her once, years ago, and the echoes would never leave her. 'I know they were the perfect couple,' she whispered. 'I know that, Sarah. I know he wouldn't look at me if she were anywhere in a thousand miles. I know—just don't say any more.'

Sarah shook her head. 'It's—this compulsion he has for you. It's . . . different from anything I've seen in him before.'

'You're imagining things.'

Sarah did not deny it.

David was standing when Julie came back. 'Ready? Shall we head off?'

'Yes.'

Compulsion? What if it was true? Did he feel the same thing she felt? Needing her, unable to stay away.

He closed the door, shutting them outside together. The moon was bathing the trees with soft light. It was a beautiful night, quiet and still.

He asked, 'Do you want to walk back?'

She nodded. 'But what about your truck?'

'I can get it tomorrow. How about your shoes?'

'They're all right if we stay on the road.'

They walked a few inches apart from each other, along the gravel drive to the road. As they turned on to McNaughton Road, David took Julie's hand, and she let her fingers curl around his.

'Are those frogs I can hear?'

'Hm,' he agreed. 'They're over in the dug-out.'

'The dug-out? What's that?'

'The watering pond in the middle of the field over there.'

She tried to remember if the pond had been there when she was a child. 'Did you make it with the bulldozer, or is it natural?'

'I made it.' His fingers settled more closely around hers. 'It fills up with water in the rainy season, in the winter. By this time of year there's not much water left in it, just enough to keep the frogs happy.'

'They must be monster frogs. They sound the size of Kermit!'

He laughed, squeezing her hand. 'You'll have to meet Molly. The first time Pat brought her over to the farm, she sat down with Sally and Jeremy and started drawing dinosaurs in amongst my cows.'

'I like her dinosaurs.'

'They're not hers alone. She does the illustrations, and some college friend of hers does the writing. He lives in Mexico and she's on Gabriola. They collaborate by mail.'

'Sounds impossible.'

'It works.' David gave a gentle tug on her hand and brought her closer, slipping his arm around her so that their thighs bumped together gently as they walked. 'Lots of things you'd never expect to work can turn out OK.'

Her heart slammed into her rib cage. Like Julie and David? Was that what he meant? Did she want this to go on and on? Weekends with David?

Yes.

Weekends, summers, whatever she could have. She forced her shoulders to relax, knowing he would feel any change in her, would sense her tension. Compulsion, Sarah had said. If David felt that kind of over-whelming need, he hid it well.

'Is that a deer?' she whispered.

'Hm.'

He stopped walking. They stood together, his arm around her as they watched the long-legged golden animal standing in the road in front of them. The deer was motionless, caught in moonlight, poised for action. After a moment of motionless preparation, it leapt suddenly, clearing the fence into David's pasture.

'Magic,' Julie whispered. The magic was here, with David. Her arm slipped around his waist and they walked slowly, tangled together.

'Julie, why didn't you and Tom have children?'

What did Tom have to do with now, with her and David?

'He said I was too young and . . .' She lifted her shoulders and felt his arm around her. She had been seventeen, a runaway bride, and Tom had probably been right about her youth. She said, 'After a few years, I wasn't so sure we should.'

He caught her hands and she was standing, staring up at his face in moonlight. He said, 'You'd make a terrific mother. Your kids would grow up with a magic kingdom for their own.'

'There's more than that to being a mother.' She wetted her lips with her tongue.

'More than love and magic? I don't think so.' His words were whimsical, almost non-sense. She frowned, and he insisted, 'Why didn't you have children later? Didn't you want them?'

'Yes.'

'But?'

Her fingers clenched on his. 'I wasn't sure they'd have a father around.'

'Why?'

'He was having other women.'

David's fingers tightened. 'Any man who had you—— Why didn't you leave him?'

'I... don't really know.'

He said, 'You didn't want to admit you'd been wrong? Stubborn, aren't you?'

'A bit.'

'A bit?' He laughed softly. 'Come here, damn you. Kiss me. I've been aching for you.'

She went into his arms in the shadows of the veranda. Her lips parted and his came down, taking possession, leaving her weak and trembling. When he swung her up, she clung to his shoulders, feeling his strength, wanting his loving with an aching only he could assuage.

Somehow he got the door to the house open without letting her go. He pushed it closed behind them with a nudge of his shoulder.

'David——'

His lips found hers in the darkness inside the house, and she could feel his heart beating strong as he held her close in his arms. When he dragged his mouth away from hers, he moved towards the stairs.

'Not upstairs, David...please——'

'Why not?' he asked simply.

'Let me down,' she whispered, but when he freed her she moved back into his arms. She could feel his hands holding her hips, eyes knowing her even in darkness.

'Why not, Julie?'

'Because——'

Upstairs there would be memories for him. She would lose, competing with Sandy's ghost. She slid her arms around his neck. Her fingers glided through the crisp, dark waves of his hair. She could feel his indrawn breath and knew this was her only chance to reach the place he kept locked away from her. She lifted herself up, her arms tight around his neck. His lips met hers. She drew him inside her, shuddering, letting her body free to strain against his.

His arms hardened, and she could feel him drawing her towards the stairs.

'No,' she whispered. She pressed close. 'Please, David...here...on...the hearthrug.'

His face was harsh in the glow of moonlight from the window. 'It's damned near public property, this house. Anyone could come in.'

She buried her face in his shoulder and whispered, 'Lock the door, then.'

He laughed, holding her against him so that she gasped at the hard pressure of his desire. 'Are you crazy? Everyone in the family has keys.'

'Then let's go to the hayloft.'

'You *are* crazy!'

She pulled back from him, felt his eyes on her, although there was only the echo of moonlight in here. 'You've slept in the loft before.'

'Slept—yes.' He moved towards her. 'We're not children now. You don't need *sleep* any more than I do. Stop running, Julie.'

If she was running, it was only symbolic. She was frozen, waiting for his touch, aching and raging with a fever only David could rouse in her. 'What's the matter?' she whispered. 'Afraid of a little adventure?'

She could see nothing but shadows in his face. He moved. Angry? Impatient? 'Who's afraid?' he growled. 'Come here.' His hand reached out, fingers seeking.

'No,' she pleaded, knowing his touch would defeat her. She turned and fled, heart tumbling, breath short.

'Julie——'

From the front door, she called back, 'Catch me if you can, David McNaughton! I always could run faster than you!'

The moon showed her the way—across the veranda, down the stairs, along the road that led to the hollow. He might have let her win as a child, but now... The dogwood tree was down there, but she rushed past it. She could feel David behind her, his shoes quieter than hers. She had no chance in a race with her skirt and low-heeled shoes, and he caught her just inside the barn. She turned and spun into his arms, warm and eager, so that he gasped as she came tight against him.

'You're crazy,' he growled, his hands on her shoulders, his breath coming unevenly there in the darkness. 'You'll ruin your clothes up there.'

'I don't care,' she said huskily. 'I don't give a damn about my clothes.' She pulled out of his arms and followed the beam of light that showed her the way to the ladder that went up.

'You're a witch.' His voice was strained.

'But you want me?' she demanded, heart frightened, voice trembling. She stopped with her back against the ladder. He caught a rung over her head with his hand, bent down and buried his face in the soft flesh at the side of her neck. She clenched her hands on the sides of the ladder behind her, tilted her head back to give him access, felt the wildness turning her breathing ragged.

'A wild woman,' he said harshly, his free hand finding her shoulder, sliding down her arm to coax her hand free of its grip on the ladder.

'Yes,' she breathed, because, whatever Sandy had been to him, it had not been wildness.

He turned his head and took her earlobe into his mouth. 'Do you expect me to carry you up that ladder?'

Julie laughed breathlessly, freed her hand from his, dragged it across his chest and felt the tension wound too tightly. 'I can get up on my own.'

He caught her ankle as she was going up, and she stopped and looked down. There was nothing to see, just blackness, and he released her. Upstairs, she opened the door that let in the moon. Then he was behind her, his arms on her shoulders.

'Julie . . .'

'What's this door thing called?' she queried nervously. 'Where you load in the hay. That's what it's for, isn't it?'

He drew her back against his hard chest, slid his hands down until they cradled her breasts.

'David, what do you call it?'

She could hardly breathe. Her voice a whisper, worth nothing. His thumbs moved up over the peaks of her breasts. Through her sweater and bra she felt the sensation as a wildness, heat in her veins.

She whispered, 'If you let me go, I'm going to fall down.'

'Good.' His hands firmed on her. 'Turn around, Julie.'

She turned, and his lips were there. She met them, clung to his shoulders with her arms, felt dizziness as he lowered her to the soft cushioning. She expected the scratchy hay, but felt softness instead. David had put something down for her. A blanket?

She laughed breathlessly. He was blocking out the light of the moon, a dark shape over her. She was lying on something soft, dragging in the wonderful aroma of clean hay. 'It smells wonderful,' she said breathlessly.

'Romantic?' he asked. He sat beside her, his weight rested on one arm as he bent over her. He touched her face, spread his fingers, traced the curve of her cheek, the angle of her jaw. Down past the trembling flesh of her throat to the curves below. He heard her indrawn breath as he traced the shape of her full breast, but went on, seeking the softness of her midriff, his hand coming to rest on the curve of her hip, fingers curved to fit her.

'Did you go to the doctor?' His voice was quiet, steady.

'Yes,' she whispered.

He said harshly, 'If you're planning to say no to me...'

She reached up and touched his chest, sliding her fingers through the gap between two buttons. She could feel the scratchy firmness of his chest hair, the hard pounding of his heart.

She wetted her lips nervously with her tongue. 'If you want me, I'm yours.'

He asked tonelessly, 'What would you do if I gave you a child?'

Her fingers dug into his arms. 'What would...what would *you* do?'

'Marry you.'

She closed her eyes painfully. Marry her. But he had made certain that she had been to the doctor. She must not cry. No matter what, tears would be a mistake. She managed somehow to say steadily, 'That would be a high price for a roll in the hay, wouldn't it?'

His head blocked the moonlight as his lips came to take hers. She found the buttons of his shirt with trembling fingers, felt the rough softness of the curling hairs on his chest. Her sweater was all buttons, a series of them parting under his touch. Then there was only her bra, and his kiss, his breath hot on her through the lace.

She heard the whimper that was her own need. She twisted in his arms and he had her bra free, pushing her sweater down her arms, his hands coming back to lift her full breasts for his kiss.

'I...David...' She could not breathe, could hardly think, only feeling, sensation. She rolled her head on the hay, found her hands locked on his shoulders, her face turning, lips seeking. When her kiss closed on his small, male nipple she heard his gasp and deepened her caress.

He pulled her away, covered her mouth with his, sliding his hands down to seek the edge of her skirt, sensuous caressing back along the nylon-clad length of her leg under the skirt. Then he bent and took her nipple into his mouth, licking softly against the hyper-sensitive nerves.

When her hand strayed to his belt, he drew it away. She twisted out of his arms, trembling in the night air.

He reached for her, but she pulled away.

'Not like that,' she whispered. 'Making me need you...and you all locked in. Why do you want to make love to me if you can't trust me that much?'

Silence, staring at him without light to see. Cool air on her naked flesh. Somewhere outside a cow made a long, plaintive noise that echoed into nothing.

David said harshly, 'Everything about you terrifies me... I—— Oh, damn it, woman! Come back here, into my arms.'

He found her tears with his lips, kissed them away, drew her hands to his chest and placed them there, whispering, 'God knows where this will end.' Then he bent to take her sweetness in his mouth.

Wild and sweet, beyond control—her touch, his kiss. Her skirt, gone with an intimate caress that made her cry his name in a shaken groan. His hands on the sleek skin of her stockings. His belt. The low groan in his throat while she touched him, her gasp when he found the hot, moist centre of her.

She wanted to melt into him, to drown in his touch. Her touch, his. Sensation, loving, needing, his need driving hers beyond all limits.

He whispered her name, then the sound turned to a groan of need and she moved to absorb the raging hunger in him, her wild blood pounding, surging with his, her gasps mingled with his groans, her body tangled with his, his caresses whispered against her heated flesh, tasting her everywhere, leaving her gasping and crying and begging for what only he could give her.

The stars exploded when he possessed her. She felt his need deep inside her, and the words he groaned were part of the night, the loving. She carried them to the place where the skies went spinning, the moon a pale white streak through the universe.

Much later, he found the corner of the blanket and pulled it over their tangled bodies. 'You're magic,' he whispered. 'Did you know that?'

She closed her eyes and breathed in the mingled scent of her lover and the fresh hay. He slid a lazy caress along the curve of her hip, turned his head and bent to bury his face in the softness of her breasts. 'Most haylofts don't feel like this,' he murmured, his lips seeking through the softness, finding what he sought. 'Do you know what you do to me?' he demanded with sudden harshness.

She turned, cradled his face with her hands and brought his lips to hers. She said unsteadily, 'I know what you do to me.'

He took her lips in small, sensuous bites. He felt her smile with his lips, moved his hand in a slow, sensuous exploration. She trembled and he asked huskily, 'Cold?'

She almost laughed, but the laughter turned to heat. His hands moved gently, tauntingly, rousing her to whispers and gasps. 'You're a witch,' he groaned when she moved against him, touching him with her new knowledge of his body, driving his slow exploration into heated need. 'Did anyone ever tell you that they burn witches?'

'Burn me, then,' she whispered, closing her eyes, taking him inside her, telling herself this was enough forever.

But later, when he was sleeping in her arms, she remembered the harshness of his voice as he had said the words, 'Marry you,' and she knew that dreams lasted only until morning.

CHAPTER NINE

'I WAS going to suggest we go down to Victoria,' said David, eyeing the sky. He turned back from the loft door, smiling down at Julie. He was wearing only his jockey shorts over the dark, muscular body that took her breath away.

She made a fair attempt at a normal voice. 'Why Victoria?'

'Stanley's performing at a night-club down there. Mom and Dad went down to see him, and I thought we'd go watch him, but maybe we'll try next week. Driving over the Malahat in a blazing rainstorm isn't exactly the way I'd most like to spend the day.'

Julie sat up, flushing at the look in David's eyes. She was twisted in that soft blanket he had produced from somewhere, but his eyes told her he knew what was under the soft covering.

'Turn around,' she whispered. 'I'll get dressed.'

He laughed softly and moved towards her, his shadow blanking out the wall of rain outside. 'I know a cure for early morning shyness,' he told her in a husky voice. He kneeled down and bent towards her, his fingers urging her lips up to his as the sound of an engine intruded.

'Someone's coming,' she said, hardly hearing her own words.

'Damn! That'll be the vet.' He closed his eyes, then said roughly, 'He was supposed to be here on Thursday, doing inoculations, but something came up. He—I've got to go down to him.'

'Go, then.' She smiled.

His eyes seemed to find the uncertainty in her eyes. 'Julie——'

A loud voice called from somewhere outside. 'David? You around?'

'Coming! Just a minute!' He held her eyes. 'I've got to go.'

'I know.' She moved to him, and he pulled her close in a hard kiss that left them both breathless. Then he pulled on his jeans and sweater and ran a rough hand through his hair as he disappeared down the ladder.

Julie dressed quickly. This morning her skirt and sweater seemed wildly impractical for what she could see outside—rain and mud, a dingy, overcast day. But last night David had held her in his arms as if he would never let her go, taking her with him to places sweet and breathless beyond her imagining.

David and the vet were nowhere in sight when she came down. She ran through the wet drive, splashing mud on her shoes, her head bowed against the rain. She should have brought that blanket, slung it over her head. She giggled, knowing how she must look, dishevelled and love-kissed, running in from the hayloft in the morning.

'Definitely incriminating,' she muttered, slamming the kitchen door behind her. She put on coffee first, because surely David would come looking for some soon. Then she went upstairs and found her weekend case in the guest-room. She sang disjointed scraps of a love song she had heard on the radio as she showered. Then she changed into jeans and brand new trainers and brushed her freshly shampooed hair into submission. She had almost had it cut short in the heat of the summer. She brushed it lovingly now, so glad she'd left it long. She closed her eyes and felt David's hands threading through her long curls, his shaken whisper telling her how much he loved her hair.

When she was done brushing, she stared at herself in the mirror. She could see it on her lips, her flushed cheeks, the light in her eyes. She loved him, deep and shattering and forever. She closed her eyes and felt his arms around her again. She heard the sound of a door downstairs and knew it was her lover.

He was in the kitchen, pouring himself a cup of coffee. His hair was curling with the rain, his jacket damp, and his lips curved as she came into the kitchen.

'Coffee,' he said, lifting the cup. 'You're an angel.'

'I've heard you say differently.' She came to him, close, and whispered, 'You've called me a brat, a little devil...'

'A witch,' he murmured, slipping his free hand into her hair. 'And you don't want to kiss me until I've finished with the vet and had a shower. There's a Thermos in the cupboard under the sink. Could you fill it for me?'

She nodded. She would do anything for him. 'What about breakfast?'

'Later. Joe needs me back there, but I'll take some coffee back with me.'

She got out the Thermos and filled it. 'After the vet, will there be time to go to Victoria? I think we should go.'

'Stanley's not expecting us.' He drained his cup. 'I talked to him Thursday night, told him I'd come down next weekend. I just thought we might surprise him if it was a nice day.'

She frowned, concentrating on the tab of a zip on his jacket. 'I don't want him to feel I'm coming between him and his father.'

He put his cup down. 'Why should he?'

'He already doesn't approve of us. That day——'

'He's a kid.' David spoke with thinly masked impatience. 'Tunnel vision. He thought things would never change for anyone but him. He's had time to adjust.'

'I don't think——'

'Don't worry about it, Julie.' He picked up the Thermos from the counter. 'You have a relationship with *me*, not my son.'

She frowned at the closing door. Not my son—as if she wasn't really a part of his life. She shivered and turned away. She had known all along that he wanted her in his arms, not his life. It was just that after last night, she had almost believed...

'Don't be a bloody fool!' she muttered. Nothing would come of yearning for more than he could give. Was she such a fool that she'd demand everything, end up with nothing?

She spread out her marking on David's desk. He kept a very tidy office. She opened the drawers and everything was there, ordered and in its place—ledgers, files, invoices sorted by category, records of inspections and government forms she hadn't dreamed existed. He'd had the bad luck to be selected as part of the sample for a detailed Statistics Canada survey of seed-stock breeding. She found the evidence of it in his drawers— copies of his quarterly survey reports neatly arranged in labelled folders.

Tidy, orderly, methodical. Where could she ever fit in all that? Who kept *copies* of StatsCan surveys, for heaven's sake? Did he have a copy of his last Canada Census form too? She couldn't even remember filling hers out.

He had always fought against her impulsive, instinctive behaviour. How many times had he told her she was a fool for leaping into things and the consequences be hanged? It didn't seem to matter when he made love to her. He wanted her to be impulsive then, deliberately roused her passions until he knew she was beyond reason. But not in the daylight. He didn't want feelings ruling in the rest of his life. He did not want her worrying about a relationship with his son, wanted to keep her in whatever compartment he'd assigned to her. She stared at the files and wondered if he would make one for her. Julie. Where would he file her? Under J for Julie? L for lover? T for temporary?

She closed the drawers with a bang. She was not going to question and worry and dread the end. It was crazy, anyway. She did not want to be a farm wife, holding on to calves and mucking out the chickens. She had a job and she belonged in the city, the last place anyone would ever find David McNaughton living.

She made certain that every drawer was closed. She had no business snooping through his files. Would he be angry if he knew? Suppressed anger, in his eyes, but not his voice. She gritted her teeth and made herself sort through the student papers on *Hamlet*.

There had been nothing suppressed last night, in his arms. His voice in her ear, trembling and shaken, carrying her with him beyond the dreams.

Oh, God! Somehow, she must shake off those dreams.

Hamlet.

She was amazed at what they thought up to re-write the master's story. She had to concentrate on that, because there would be more times like this. Uncertainty and longing. She would have to learn to carry on with the rest of her life between...between—— She was *not* running away this time. If it hurt, then it was pain she would have to live with. Whatever it was that she had going with David, he would have to be the one to say it was over.

She managed to smile as she read the first version of how Shakespeare should have straightened out the indecisive Dane's behaviour. She was deep in the third version by the time the telephone at her elbow rang.

'Hello?' she said absently, reading Edie's version of how Hamlet should have dealt with Ophelia's death. 'McNaughton Farm,' she added belatedly.

'Julie? It's Sarah.'

'Oh, hi! I——'

'Would you tell David to get down to the south pasture right away? That damned bull's gone through the fence again. The Terrance boy was going by on a motorcycle and got charged.'

'Is he OK?'

Sarah laughed. 'Sure. Terrified, but he's got a story for his friends. I don't know that the bull *really* charged—scared the kid witless, though. Just tell David to get the bull off the damned road before I have to go into town for Sally's ballet practice. Edward says he'll come along, but he'll need David there to tell him what to do.'

Julie grabbed a jacket she found hanging in the mud-room and threw it over her blouse. She found David and a swarthy, muscular man of around fifty bending over a calf under a shelter in the corral.

'David!' She stopped, panting slightly from her mad dash. 'Sarah says your bull's gone through the fence in the south pasture. He's on the road!'

'Hell!' muttered David, keeping his grip on the calf.

'OK,' said the vet, 'she's done. You can let her go.'

Both men stood up, avoiding the calf's scramble to get free of them with the ease of long practice. 'I'll give a hand with the bull if you want,' offered the vet.

'Thanks,' said David. 'Let's go, then.' He threw back at Julie, 'This would have wiped out Victoria in any case. I'll have to have a look at that fence.'

'Sarah said Edward would come down to help.'

David nodded abruptly and headed for the pick-up truck. Julie saw him throw a rope into the back, heard him call something back to the vet.

David and the vet. Edward too. Three men, and how was it you got a bull to go back inside a fence he'd escaped? If a yearling weighed fourteen hundred pounds, what about a full-grown bull? She remembered that day Patrick had dared her to cut through the bull pen, remembered staring at the fierce animal as it swung to look at her, nostrils flaring with irritation. David, grabbing her roughly and sweeping her out of the enclosure, shouting, 'You bloody fool! You could have been killed! Don't you ever think first?'

She went back to the farmhouse. How often did this kind of thing happen? She stared at the closed cupboards in the kitchen and re-alised that he hadn't even had breakfast. Sandy would never have let him go out in the morning without breakfast. Sandy, who'd intimidated even Sarah with her efficiency.

She found a cold roast in the refrigerator and made sandwiches. Lots of them, because it might not be only David when they returned. She piled the plate high and covered them all with plastic wrap. She would heat up tinned soup when they came back. She supposed Sandy would have had a big pot simmering, real home-made soup. Julie had not been in this kitchen more than two or three times when it was Sandy's domain, but she thought there had always been the smell of something delicious brewing.

She rinsed the bread knife and the butcher knife. Did David put them in the dishwasher? Had Sandy used that dishwasher when...? She had to stop this! Must not let herself think and wonder.

When David had his arms around her, his lips on hers, did he want it to be Sandy in his arms?

She went back to the office, but it was no good, completely unfair to any students who would be victims of her marking with this pain in her heart. She knew she could not be jealous of a dead woman. It was wrong. It was more than that. Crazy, because... Julie shuddered and tried not to do it, but she went up the stairs.

Into David's room. It had been Sandy's room too. Mr and Mrs McNaughton had moved into the guest house when David married Sandy. And this was the master bedroom.

Julie stopped when she found it.

Not on his bedside table, thank God! On the dresser. You could not tell from the picture that she was tall and slender, but Julie could close her eyes and remember. In the picture she had long, straight blonde hair, although Julie remembered it shorter. But the smile was the same. Julie remembered the smile. She had never realised until now, looking at the image of Sandy McNaughton, that it was the kind of smile a man might dream of. David must dream of it. A woman like that would cook wonderful meals, smile patiently when her child turned irritating and temperamental. She would know how to handle her man without turning to temper and messy skirmishes.

That was not what Sarah had said. Sarah had said that David had dominated Sandy. Julie swallowed and knew it must have been what he wanted. How often had he told Julie she should be different?

The woman in the picture would welcome a man to her bed with warm, slender arms and that smile turned intimate and...that bed. Julie closed her eyes. She had averted it last night, had known she could not lie there with him. Somehow, she had managed to draw David down to the barn where there were no memories to compete with. But tonight...

Last night she had thought...but he still kept her picture in his room. Every morning, he woke to see her first, before anything else.

Julie went slowly downstairs.

They all came back together, hungry and noisy, dirty and wet from the pouring rain outside. 'We'll wash first,' said David, glancing at the pile of hungry eyes and steering them all back to the washroom off the mud-room.

Julie had the soup ready when they came to the table with clean faces and hands. David and Edward and—amazingly—Patrick.

'Hi, stranger,' said Pat as he sat down at the table. 'God, this looks good! Learned to cook, did you, over the years?'

'Given a good can-opener,' she tossed back, but David would be remembering Sandy, who hadn't needed to turn to a can for a good meal. 'I thought they got rid of you,' she teased Pat. Anything to keep from looking at David's eyes. 'Tossed you out of the country.'

'You heard it wrong. I had to run away to get a bit of privacy with my new wife.'

'I love eating other people's food,' said Edward, sitting down beside Patrick. 'My wife never cooks me a decent meal.'

'She'll murder you in your bed one day,' said David. There was laughter in his eyes.

'Don't believe Edward,' muttered Pat around a mouthful of sandwich. 'The first time Molly met him, she was looking after Sarah's kids. Sarah had gone into hospital to have the twins. Edward's a graduate chef, and he had poor Molly conned into thinking he couldn't open a can. She was cooking and washing and——' He laughed. 'Sarah just about killed him when she learned he'd let Molly do all that!'

'Congratulations,' said Julie. 'I hear Molly's something special.'

'Thanks,' he said huskily. 'She's more than special.' He was the same tease she remembered, laughter in his eyes and that stubborn determination hidden behind. But when he said Molly's name, his voice softened and the love showed through.

Her eyes got caught in David's. Later, his were saying. Julie turned away to the stove, asked, 'More soup, anyone?'

'Me, please,' said David, and she felt uncomfortably self-conscious as she filled his bowl, knowing he was watching, wondering if he was comparing this with other memories.

Outside, wheels crunched on the drive. 'That'll be Molly,' said Pat. 'Come to take me to the ferry.' He got up and greeted her as she came through the doorway, sweeping her into his arms.

Molly was flushed as she emerged from her husband's embrace. She had an arresting face, greenish eyes, curly black hair tied back from her face with a plain red piece of cloth.

David said warmly, 'Welcome back, Molly. I won't hug you till later—I was a lot closer to the bull than Pat was.'

'Did you catch the cow?' asked Molly.

'Caught and penned,' said Patrick. 'And I could swear I remember David's vowing he'd never let me near his cattle again.'

David was leaning back in his chair, eyes amused as he said drily, 'A man's got to be flexible. You've matured a little since you were a teenager—feeding junk to the cows, daring Julie to sneak through the bull pen.'

Pat winced. 'I didn't know you'd found out about that. I honestly didn't think she'd do it. Julie, you swore you wouldn't tell!'

Julie said, 'That sort of promise is only good for a few years. For poetic justice, though, that cow should have charged you today.'

'That would have completely ruined the effect,' said Pat.

Molly laughed, her green eyes taking light. 'We should get this into the newspaper: political hopeful saves Gabriolan cow.'

'Bull,' corrected David.

Pat said wryly, 'I was nothing more than wallpaper on this job. You should have seen it, Molly. David just walks up to the darned bull, as cool as usual. El Toro is staring through the neighbour's fence at the cows, so he turns and eyes David and makes one of those bull-type snorts. So David says, ''Come on, they're not worth it,'' and he puts the rope through the ring in the bull's nose. And that's the end of it. The rest of us just watched, and helped mend the fence afterwards.'

David said, 'If Pat really does run for MLA, we can fake the story. Gabriolan pacifies raging bull—something like that. Molly, this is Julie Charters. Belated introductions.'

Molly reached a slender hand to greet Julie. 'Hi, Julie. I'll have to get you to tell me all Pat's darkest secrets from his childhood.'

Julie shook her head. 'I was only a summer visitor, summers and holidays. Would you like some soup, Molly?'

'Oh, no, thanks. I just had a massive lunch at Sarah's. I've been eating like a pig lately.' Julie saw Molly's eyes meet her husband's and something warm passed between them.

'Are you getting any marking done?' David asked Julie.

'Some. I'm about half done.'

Pat said with mock amazement, 'David tells me you're a teacher now. Julie keeping a bunch of teenaged troublemakers in line? I can just see it——'

David said, 'She wraps them around her finger. When she walks into the classroom, they stop breathing.'

She wished David would stop watching her. She needed time—hours, perhaps days or weeks. Time to find a mask for it all, to be able to turn to David, to go into his arms without it all spilling out. All the things she could never say, questions she could never ask.

The men demolished the pot of soup and all the sandwiches but one, leaving it as lone evidence that she had made enough. When Molly said to Pat, 'If you really want to catch that ferry...?' he nodded and got up quickly.

'I'm off. Back home for a shower, then would you believe I've got to go into the office? Three months and they survived with only contact by modem, and now the whole system's falling apart. While I'm in town, I'll pick up the 'vette.' Patrick caught Molly's hand in his. 'Are you going back, Edward? Want a ride?'

Edward said, 'Thanks. Yes.'

Molly smiled at Julie. 'Come on over later, if you can. Or tomorrow, how about dinner? Bring David, and we'll all have a barbecue.'

'We'll see,' said David, then they drove away in Molly's small van, leaving quiet behind.

Julie moved restlessly to pick up their dirty dishes. 'What happened to the vet?'

David turned away from the door, where he'd been watching the van drive away. 'He went on home, wanted to catch the next ferry.'

'What made the cow break loose?'

'Bull,' he corrected, 'not cow. I think it was the thunder that spooked him.'

'I didn't hear thunder.' She had been in the office, she supposed, trying to work on marking while David and the vet were down with the calves.

'There was some. Nothing much, but he doesn't like it much. It's miserable out there, blowing and sleeting. You'd think he'd stand under a tree, but...'

Julie stacked the bowls in the dishwasher, then added the spoons. 'Isn't it risky?' She turned back in time to see his shrug. He would not tell her if it was dangerous, she supposed. David always had to have everything in control, and of course he would be careful. 'Does it happen very often?'

'Now and then,' he said, which wasn't any answer at all.

'What about your hired hand? Can't he look after it?'

'He's off this weekend—gone down to visit his parents in Sooke.'

She came back to the table with a cloth, but he took it away from her. 'Stop it, Julie! The lunch was great, but I didn't invite you here to tie you to an apron. Go back to your marking; I'll finish this clearing up.'

'I——' She stared at the cloth. She wanted to take it back, finish the job she had started, wanted to tell him not to shut her out of his kitchen, his relationship with his son, his life.

David said, 'I've got to go out to feed the chickens. That got forgotten, what with the great bull escape.' He was chuckling, then suddenly quiet. 'After that, I'll come in and have a shower.'

She swallowed, meeting his eyes. After the shower...

He asked, 'How long will the marking take?'

'About another hour.' She touched the tip of her tongue to her dry lips.

'OK.' He smiled. 'Go get it done, then.'

She said stiffly, 'Molly's pregnant. Did you know that?'

'Pat didn't say anything.' David shook his head sceptically. 'How could you know? Sarah told you?'

'Just the way they looked at each other, when she made that comment about eating so much.' She had watched that look between Molly and Patrick, had felt the empty pain of knowing it would never be her, never David's eyes telling love and secrets only for Julie.

'Guesswork,' said David.

'Want to bet on it?'

He laughed. 'Not on your life! You've a horrible knack of winning bets. I'll ask Pat.'

Julie laughed, moving towards the study, thinking maybe it would be all right. He caught her as she was walking past him, pulled her to him and took her lips in a possessive kiss. 'Just so you remember,' he said in a low voice as he released her.

She pulled back, and could see the laughter in his eyes. 'Lord, woman,' he demanded huskily, 'how can you be shy after last night?'

She shook her head. 'I'm not exactly——'

'Not in my arms,' he agreed, and her cheeks flamed.

She would never manage the marking, not with the knowledge that he would come, his arms and his lips possessing her, taking her...would he swing her up into his arms, climb those stairs? Could she...just somehow close her eyes and pretend that...

She put a red circle around a word on a
page of stage directions. *Hamlet* had been
played on a simple set with few props. Clut-
tering up purity of lines and emotion with a
bunch of artificial props wouldn't...

She heard David's feet on the stairs, going
up. To that room, then the shower. She could
hear the water faintly. He would have stripped
off in the bathroom that led off the master
bedroom. Had Sandy gone in there some-
times while he was showering, handing him a
towel as he stepped out, going into his arms
when he pulled her against his wet, hard
body?

She had to stop this! It was sick, being
jealous of a woman who was gone. There was
no way she could ever explain this to David,
no way she would find anything but anger in
his eyes if she tried. And it wasn't all his years
with Sandy that she minded. It was now, the
terrible conviction that he would rather have
another woman in his arms, his bed, his life.

She heard him walking overhead, out of the
shower. Was he naked? Covered, with a towel
wrapped around his waist? What was that
sound? Drawers. The dresser. Could he see
her picture now? She closed her eyes and there

was silence overhead. Nothing. He would be looking at the image of Sandy, wishing...

Her fingers clenched when she heard his feet on the stairs, coming down.

'Finished?' he asked, coming into the office. His office, the one room in this house that she felt had no shadows. She supposed that was why she had spread out her things here, trying to stake some kind of stupid claim.

'Yes,' she said in a low voice, 'finished.' It had hardly started. Breathless loving, hiding from the shadows.

David came into the room, hands resting on the far side of the desk, leaning towards her. 'Are you going to put it away?'

She nodded, saw her hands moving, stacking up the papers. His eyes, watching her. Waiting for the papers to be gone before he touched her. Her briefcase at the side of the desk. He picked it up and she handed him the little stack of papers. He slid them inside.

'That all?'

'Yes.'

Better if she said it now, with the desk between them. She didn't know what the words were, but easier to find them now then later. He put the briefcase down without looking, his eyes fixed on her face. He bent across the desk and she watched the muscles of his forearm thicken as he leaned towards her. He brushed his lips on hers.

He murmured, 'Could I talk you into some music? Some logs burning in the fireplace? A warm retreat on a rainy day?'

She nodded. He held out his hand and led her into the living-room. She sat down on the sofa, frozen, watching him at the fireplace. His back was broad and strong, a soft sweat-shirt stretched across his shoulders. She would remember the feel of his back always, firm cool ridges of muscle under her fingers. The dark hairs that curled against the back of his neck, so much softer than the crisp waves that fell over his forehead. She had been insane to think it could work. Underneath, she must have known. Why else bring her own car when the bus would be so much easier? She had known she was only reaching for dreams, illusions. A child looking at treasures through a shop window had more chance of fantasy coming true.

He came to her when the logs were crackling with new yellow flames. He sat beside her on the sofa and took her in his arms, drawing her across his lap to cradle her against his chest.

'I forgot the music,' he said, bending to taste her mouth with his.

She swallowed. He brushed her lips apart. 'I can't,' she breathed. The words hardly escaped, but she heard their echo and her own heart drummed into the silence.

'Did you think I'd make a love slave of you?' he teased gently. 'Just let me hold you. I want you in my arms.'

She turned her face into his throat, felt the warm smell of his own personal man's scent mixed with soap. He drew her closer and she could have stayed there forever, silence and closeness.

'That's not what I mean,' she whispered. 'I...' She moved away and his arm held her from falling, his thighs hard under her buttocks, his eyes narrowed, watching her, perhaps finally sensing something.

'What exactly *do* you mean?'

She stared at the deep cleft of his chin, knew she must not let her fingers slip up to explore it. She focused on his chin, the firm lips, straight, waiting. She said slowly and steadily, 'I can't go upstairs with you. Sooner or later, this is going to lead there, isn't it?

Making love, upstairs, in your—— And I can't do that. Not ever.'

Silence. Not the David of last night, taking her with passions unleashed and voice trembling with need. This was the other David, thinking before he said anything.

Then, 'Why not?'

She stared at his lips. No softness there. What had Patrick said about Molly? More than special, and that light in his eyes when he looked at her——

David's eyes were shuttered and hard.

Julie moved away stiffly, and he let her go. She realised, too late, that if there was any chance of making him understand, she had to stay close, talking with touch as well as voice.

'You've always been afraid of your own emotions,' he said harshly.

She reached to touch his arm. 'That's not true! It's you that——'

He shook off her touch, tore through his still-damp hair with angry fingers. 'I've had trouble with my feelings for you. Yes, I have. I've always——'

She turned away, not wanting to listen, shutting his words out.

He pushed angrily to his feet, prowling to the fireplace. 'You know what's between us.'

She watched him pick up a glass ornament, turning it in his hands as if with anger. 'The air's thick with it. When I put my arms around you, you can't hide what you feel. But you haven't the guts to reach out, to—— When you're not in my arms, you spend all your time denying that there's anything between us.'

'I don't.'

His grip tightened cruelly on the ornament. 'You haven't the guts to face your own emotions honestly.'

'It's not—not that.'

'What, then?' he demanded bitterly.

Julie closed her eyes and turned away from him. The fire still burned on her lids. She could feel her own words empty on the stillness of the room. 'It isn't me you really want. You didn't want me years ago, when I asked you. You wanted her. And now, you still wouldn't, not if she were here. I'm second best, and when you touch me, I—— If you touch me, take me, into that room, that bed, I'll know it's really her you want, that I'm only—you're . . . wishing I were her. If she weren't dead——'

She swallowed, hearing the echo of her own words. 'I don't believe I said that,' she whispered. 'But it's true. That's how I feel.' She turned around, made herself face him. She had never seen his eyes quite like that, flat and dark and sad. She whispered, 'If she were here, we'd never have happened.'

'No,' he agreed.

She swallowed. 'So...I...I'd better go, hadn't I?'

David stared at the glass gripped in his hand. 'Running? Always running.' He walked away from her, to the window, staring out at the darkness that could almost have been night. A rainy, sad day. 'Sandy's a fact, Julie. She was my wife for fifteen years. I loved her.'

She stared at his back.

'All right,' he said suddenly, harshly, 'so it's a problem between us. Can't you face it, come to terms with it?' He spun around so fast that she jerked back. 'Is it easier to walk out and go it alone? None of us were meant to go it alone, Julie.'

'I——'

'Once you knew that, didn't you? When you were thirteen? You didn't try to shut out love then.'

She blinked tears away, then said honestly, 'I don't want to remember that. Why can't you forget it?'

'Because you've never forgotten it. It's there between us, and it's something I can never do anything about, never could. Because I wanted to be able to—you were reaching out and I loved you, but the whole thing was out of step, impossible.'

'You loved Sandy,' she said dully.

'Yes, but I was a man, Julie. Sandy was a young woman. You were a child. And I certainly couldn't love you as a man.'

She whispered, 'No more than you could ever feel for me now what you felt for her.'

David's face went harsh and still, then something exploded in him. 'What the hell do you want me to do? She was my wife. We lived in this house, yes, for years. Do you want to know how often we made love? Where?'

'No,' she whispered. 'No.'

'In this room.' He moved towards her, one angry step, then two, and Julie backed up. 'Do you want to know how often? Where Stanley was conceived? I'll tell you that if you need it. In the back of a car up on the Malahat. Is that what you want to know? And she told me she was on the Pill, but she wasn't. She did it deliberately, because she wanted to get married then, and I wanted to wait until——

Does that help? What else would you like to know? That the first time I made love to you, I wanted——'

She shook her head. 'Stop it—please!' She could feel the tears starting and she blinked, tried to stand there and somehow endure through this. She saw his hand move in an angry gesture, heard the little glass ornament smashing on the floor.

'What do you want me to do, then, Julie? Take every memory and burn it? Burn this house down? Why the hell should you be jealous of Sandy? She's dead! Why can't you just let what's between us simply *be*?'

She shook her head mutely. 'It's not like that. It's just—I just wanted—needed...'

The anger went out of him abruptly. He said in a tired voice, 'What do you want me to say, Julie? That I would have left my wife for you?'

She shook her head mutely.

His voice was granite, anger turned to ice. 'All I can say——'

'No, don't!' She brushed at the tears, but they would not stop. 'Don't say any more. I—— I just can't take any more of this! I—— Get—get out of my way...let me...please, I've got to get out.'

His jaw jerked. 'You can't take any more! Well, neither can I, Julie! Running after you. Trying to—— If you're staying, then stay; have some real guts for once in your life, stop and fight for what you want. You didn't fight for Tom, did you? Didn't care enough, I suppose.' His lips twisted in an angry smile. 'I suppose this isn't much different, although I'd thought—— If it's some kind of pure perfection you're asking of me, I can't give it. I'm a man, with a past. You're a grown woman. You should be able to—— It's not as if you've come to me a virgin, with——'

'Oh, please! Don't! Just let me go!'

He was between her and the door. She closed her eyes, wanted to scream something, knew there was nothing but pain. She turned abruptly and ran upstairs, into the guest-room. Her case, her bag. She heard the door slam downstairs, would not let herself go to the door to watch where he went. He was gone; that was all that mattered. By the time he'd returned, she would be gone too.

CHAPTER TEN

JULIE turned left at the road, not right. She would take everything, every scrap. Leave nothing behind to make her think there was a reason to go back.

She knew it was foolish, going to that cabin looking for a blouse and bra she had left behind weeks ago. Maybe David had found her things, taken them home. But—— She closed her eyes briefly, felt the car start to slide on the gravel and jerked them open. Not yet. She must not let go yet. Later, when she was off this island. When she had erased all trace. She would sell the damned house too, because she would never be able to come back.

No smoke rising from the chimney of the log cabin. Nobody here. Of course not; they were both in town. Julie braked in front of the cabin and let out a long breath, her hands clenched on the wheel as her little car trembled in a sudden gust of wind. This was absolutely insane, going into someone else's property in the midst of an autumn gale. But she did not want Molly to find the traces of clothes she had left behind. She or Pat might wonder, might ask David if——

No one would ask. It would be a mystery. But Molly might mention it to Sarah, and Sarah would put two and two together—that night when Julie had disappeared from Sarah's with David. His truck gone in the middle of the night. Had David come storming into Sarah's the next morning, demanding to know what had happened to his truck?

David didn't storm. He lost his temper only with Julie. He had said she was a witch. Perhaps, but more likely she was a sliver under his skin.

She ran from the car to the cabin, the rain pounding down on her head. Dark would come early tonight, a black night. It did not matter. Once she was off this island, nothing would matter much.

It was a well-built cabin, small and cosy. She remembered how it had been in the middle of a warm summer night, but even now there was a feeling of cosiness from the warm log walls. The sky outside was black, but in here it seemed warm. She pushed the door slowly closed behind her, felt the warmth on her cheeks, cold dampness clinging from her jeans and blouse.

Warmth—too warm for an empty cabin. Julie heard a sound and looked up. Legs, coming down the split log stairs from the loft. David had carried her up there. David... Long, slender woman's legs. Molly.

Molly stopped halfway down the stairs, looking down at Julie with an arrested expression of curiosity on her face.

'Julie! Come on up.'

'I—I thought you'd gone to town.'

'No, I just dropped Pat off at the ferry.' Molly came down four more steps—waiting, Julie supposed, for an explanation. The black and white cat called Trouble appeared at the top of the stairs, stretching.

Julie spread her hands helplessly. 'I—I just...' Why had she come? What did a blouse matter? She focused on the cat moving down the stairs. It had been a stupid notion that she could clean her identity out of here, leave the place and have nothing pulling her back.

Molly came the rest of the way down the stairs. She was now dressed in paint-stained jeans, a loose T-shirt of Patrick's, and the beginnings of a smile. Julie said desperately, 'This is a horrible day.'

'I take it you're not talking about David's loose cow?'

'His bull.' Julie grimaced at her own correction. 'This is really—I...'

'Come on up.' Molly was smiling, a faint dreaminess in her eyes. 'I'm in the middle of a dinosaur, but we'll have coffee. I just have to get Terry down on paper before I lose the idea I had.'

'Terry——? Your pterodactyl?' How did you ask this sort of thing? Excuse me, but did you come back from your honeymoon and find someone had left some clothes lying around in your loft?

'Sounds batty, doesn't it?' said Molly with a grin.

Julie jerked. 'What?'

'Talking about my dinosaurs as if they were real. To me, I guess they are. Crazy, but—— You are going to come in, aren't you? You're soaking wet! I just started the electric heat, but I could get a fire going.'

'I think I'd better go. I just came for....'

'Your things,' suggested Molly gently. 'I've collected them in a bag. I was going to give them to David to send on to you.'

'How did you know——?'

'Sarah mentioned that you and...just guesswork.' Molly turned away from Julie's flushed face. 'I'll put the coffee-pot on, shall I?'

'You must think...' Julie followed into the kitchen uneasily. 'I don't want to take you away from your dinosaurs.'

Molly was filling a kettle to put on the gas stove. She said quietly, 'Sarah thinks you've got David half out of his mind.'

'No.'

'Can you stand instant?' Molly pulled down a container from an overhead shelf. 'That's all I've got here at the moment—I don't know David all that well, but he strikes me as the sort who keeps it all locked in. I can't imagine him behaving irrationally.'

Julie rammed her fists into her jeans pockets.

Molly got out two mugs. 'You look like someone who could use a friend.'

Julie shook her head.

Molly smiled, and Julie thought she could see how this woman had found her way through Patrick's smooth polish to the heart underneath. Julie shivered and said dully, 'I've—I've got to go. I want to catch the next ferry.'

The electric light overhead flickered, then recovered. Molly glanced at it, said resignedly, 'If the power gives out in this storm, I'll have to give up on Terry. Can't paint by candlelight.' Her dreamy green eyes fixed on Julie, then sharpened suddenly. 'You were going to stay the whole weekend, weren't you? I know it's not my business, but—— That's like the echo of a bad dream. I ran away from Patrick, all the way to Ottawa. And he—— Don't go, not in this weather. It's blowing a gale. The ferry crossing will be rough.'

'No, it's too late. Too messed up for going back.' Julie hugged herself. She was not going to cry. Although, if Molly said one more sympathetic, caring word... 'If I could get my things...?'

'Why don't you stay here? I'm just using it as a studio. Your old place isn't really habitable, is it? Sarah said—maybe you could use some time alone, to think things over.'

'No, I—— Please.'

Molly shrugged, but poured the instant coffee into a polystyrene cup she found in a cupboard. 'Take this, then. It's warm. Sugar? Cream?'

Julie went out to her car with the steaming cup in one hand and a paper bag with her clothes in the other. Molly came with her, getting wet for no good reason Julie could see, except that she opened the car door for Julie and said, 'If you change your mind, the place is never locked. Just walk in and make yourself at home.'

She had once before, with David. Molly must know that, but she was too warm a person to let Julie feel uncomfortable about it. Julie put the coffee in her drinks holder and the bag in the back seat.

'Thanks. And I really am happy about you and Pat. He deserves someone nice.'

Molly said quietly, 'So does David.'

Julie shivered. David deserved someone nice, but it would not be her. He wanted a lover, not a new love, and she could not bear to live separate from what he felt deep inside, except when she was caught in his arms in passion...

It was not even night yet, but Julie found herself reaching for her headlight switch. Molly had turned lights on in the kitchen, but it was still late afternoon, the sky darkened with the storm. Julie's little car was so small that the wind kept catching it as she drove along North Road. Ten kilometres to the ferry, but it seemed forever. Trees meeting overhead, blocking out what little light there was. In daylight it was magical, driving through the trees with high branches reaching to touch hands overhead.

Not now. The wind was raging, branches swinging wildly against the dark sky. The rain had stopped, or perhaps the tall trees filtered it out.

David . . .

He had called her a coward, afraid to trust, to take a chance. He was right and wrong both at the same time. Molly had said . . . the sort who kept it all locked in. But what was locked inside David? Loving . . . could he . . . could he——

He had said he wanted all of her, not to leave any part behind. That didn't make sense, if . . . but David always made sense. David——

No more, he had said. Can't stand any more. Running after her. Trying to——what? She had to know that. His exact words were gone. She had heard only the anger, fury in his voice, the glass shattering, and David would never throw it in anger. Had to ask him——go back. How could she run from her own heart? Stay, he had said. Stay and . . . and let——

A shifting of black on black. Nothing, but Julie felt her heart stop. She jerked her foot to the brake. A deer?

Bigger! Moving...a tree, falling, falling right——

She jerked the wheel to throw the car sideways. Small car, so light. She had pulled too hard, thrown it out of control.

Branches everywhere! Dark arms crashing down.

He knew what he should have told her. He had shouted, accused her of everything from carelessness to cowardice——could never seem to keep his damned mouth under control of his brain when he was with her. But in all the shouting, even when he'd seen her tears...he had not once told her that he loved her.

Because...because, although he tried to believe she felt the same, she had spent a great deal of time and energy in telling him all the ways her future did not have a farmer in it. Back to college. Her own school. City ambitions, not the kind that made a man feel he would have a chance in hell of holding her close for the rest of his life.

Her children—— God, how he ached to see her with children—his children. Theirs. She had such a magic for kids. That class full of rowdy teenagers hanging on her words. Sarah's kids crawling all over her, and when he had seen her holding little Tammy in her arms——

Why the hell could they never simply *talk*? In her arms there had been no need for words. He had told her with his body all the things he found so hard to express. But, in words, it always turned to too much emotion, too little understanding. What the hell did a man need with this kind of torment? How could she have lain in his arms and not *known* what was in his heart? He had been walking around all day, through the bull and the fence and the vet...holding Julie close to his heart, *knowing* he had won the only woman in the world he could dream of wanting for his own.

Then, when she pulled away and accused him of substituting her for Sandy, he had felt as if she had slapped him—disorientated, shocked.

He had found Sandy's picture on his dresser when he came out of the shower earlier, had stood staring at it, wondering how long since he had actually seen it. Sweet years, but gone now. He was not the man who had been Sandy's husband. He was changed partly by his grief, partly by the simple passage of time. Different needs, desires, hungers. He'd taken the picture down into Stanley's room before he went down to Julie.

And now...her car was gone when he came slowly back to the house. He had known it would be. He stared at the pick-up in front of the farmhouse, his hands clenched into fists. She would be at the ferry. Would he be driven to pursue her all the rest of his life, trying to force her to face what was between them? He closed his eyes and knew it would be better to leave the damned thing alone now. He felt the tearing pain in his chest, turned and went into the house, slamming the door behind him. He told himself to head for the kitchen and some coffee, but his feet took him to the room where Julie's things had been.

Her case gone, bag gone. Julie gone. David's eyes fell on the clock at her bedside table...why *her* bedside table, when countless people had slept in this room over the years?

Too late to catch the ferry. He could get the next one and still catch the last ferry to Vancouver, but what then? What did she want of him? To erase Sandy? He didn't ask that of her, did he? She had mentioned Tom's name a few times, and he didn't freeze up as if——

He had, at first. Until he realised——

He went downstairs, mechanically fixed a pot of coffee. He would dust off his pilot's licence. The south pasture had once been used as a runway; it wouldn't take much to get the grass strip back in shape. This business of being stuck on Gabriola, with Julie back in Vancouver——

The pager on his belt beeped. He froze, waiting for the message.

A woman's voice crackled and announced, 'Tree down across North Road on Gabriola Island.'

David was moving down to the pick-up truck before the squelch on the pager cut off the noise. She would *have* to stop running eventually. He was damned well not going to let her hide from this thing between them forever. After the tree, he'd come back and...telephone, maybe. Try to find words.

The downed tree first. So many tall old trees on the island. North Road wound through some of the tallest, and it was not unusual for the high winds to bring one down, often taking out power lines with the tree. He had not lost electricity here on the farm, but his

power came up from the feeder on South
Road. He had a generator on the farm, because power cuts weren't uncommon during
the storms.

He checked his speed as he pulled on to the
public road. Having an accident on the way
to the fire hall wouldn't help anyone. He
glanced in the rear-view mirror and saw a
station wagon behind— Edward. They
parked side by side at the fire hall. The doors
were already open, the pumper truck warming
up. Inside, David glanced at the map.
Someone had already put the pin in at the lo-
cation. On the blackboard, it was in words:
NORTH ROAD NEAR ELGIE. TREE DOWN. CAR
REPORTED TRAPPED.

Oh, God!

David burst into the radio room, demanding, 'Got any more information?'

The volunteer on the radio looked up. 'Hi,
Captain. Guy that reported it says there's a
car caught under. Hydro line down, still live.
The chief's at the scene, west side. They can't
get near it until the power's cut. Small car.'
He shrugged. 'God knows—— Chief says can
we take the pumper and the tanker round by
Peterson. Hydro crews are on the way over—
special ferry run.'

David nodded abruptly. It could be anyone. No reason to think that Julie—— He turned back to the meeting-room. They were all there. Automatically, he began to organise them. 'Edward, you're on the pumper. Take Saul with you; I'll go with the tanker. Max, check the gear in the tanker—chain-saws, especially. Let the trucks warm up while we get our gear on.'

Was it a red car? He knew he must not take valuable radio time when he could hear the frequency busy. David got his own gear on, yellow waterproof and pants, checked his air pack. With that electric transmission line down and live...and a car underneath. Not Julie. Please, not Julie!

Two other volunteers came in. He assigned one to come in the tanker with him, the other to follow in his own vehicle. David grabbed the tanker's microphone as they started out and announced, 'Number three responding with three men.'

It was dark, the late afternoon sun well hidden by black storm-clouds. The ten-minute drive through buffeting rain seemed endless. When they turned on to North Road, David felt his eyes straining ahead. He should have stopped her, somehow...somehow—should *never* have walked out like a kid with a temper tantrum. Next time...next time they'd damn well stay in one room until they'd sorted it out. Whatever the problem was. Together.

So many small cars on this island. It would not be Julie's, caught under some tree, caught in the power line. Oh, God, Julie! Please...

Then he saw the tree—a giant, fallen diagonally across the road, the branches standing out from it in all directions, rising up perhaps twenty feet. If there was a car under all that——

The fire truck jerked to a halt and David shot out. There were three cars parked alongside the road, people who would have been on their way to the ferry, now standing in the rain. Yellow flames sparked and sputtered on the left side of the road, about ten feet up in the branches of the fallen tree.

He called back to Edward, 'Get some cones and make a barrier back from that fallen electric line. Keep everyone clear of this tree until they kill the power. Bring the truck over and block the road to stop any more cars coming up here! We'll need room to clear this away.'

The civilian at his elbow said, 'There's a car under it. You can't see it—— God, there's so many branches, but I know it's there.'

David turned and recognised a familiar face, an island resident he knew by sight. 'You saw it?'

'Yeah. I was behind it—her. A woman, with long hair. I could see her silhouette through the windows. I hope I never see one of those trees going down again. She tried to avoid...the car was going sideways, but it must have hit right on.'

David asked hoarsely, 'What kind of car? What colour?'

'Red. One of those little red things—Firefly or a Suzuki Swift. Something like that.'

David closed his eyes painfully, spoke rigidly into his hand-held radio. 'Chief? David here with number two and three in position on the east side.'

'David, how many men?'

David glanced back. 'Five, more just coming in their own cars. What's the score on the electricity?'

The chief's voice crackled. 'They promised us——' The flare of fire near the wire died to nothing. 'There it goes. Hold on—— Yeah, we've got the all clear from Hydro. They've turned off the whole island until the crews get out here. Can you give me a report on that side?'

'Give me a minute.' David shouted back, 'Edward! Saul! Let's get some lights and chain-saws up here! Just the two of you until we see what's holding that tree up.' He swallowed raw fear and said steadily to the civilian beside him, 'Get the others to clear back, could you? And pull your cars back too. We're going to need room here.'

The radio crackled. 'Can't see the car at all from this side. Can you confirm if there's really a car in there?'

'My witness says yes, but hold on. Getting lights up here!' David took the light from Edward and started to fight his way into the thick growth. As he moved ahead, the headlights from the tanker moved into position. The lights showed a giant, fallen Douglas fir, branches thick and filled with needles. They would have to start cutting to find anything much. But if there was a car in there... The witness could be wrong. Julie might somehow have got through under the tree before it——

His light caught a glimpse of red. He swung it back and there was no longer any doubt.

He swallowed terror and said rigidly into the microphone, 'Chief, David here. Confirmed on the car, but I can't get near it.' He took a jagged breath. She had to be all right. Somehow he had to get her out of there. He said tonelessly, 'It's pinned by branches, both sides and on top. The roof is—looks bad. Can you send some men around here? Saws, ambulance. You'll probably want to come yourself.'

At David's back, Edward breathed, 'It's going to take a damned big crew to clear this out.'

David said painfully, 'It's Julie.' He keyed the radio again. 'What about the ambulance?'

'On its way. He's got instructions to come round to your side.'

Could the driver of that car possibly be alive? He turned away to the other firemen, knowing he must not let himself think of that. Not now. He had to keep himself together, alert and efficient and somehow...somehow get her out of there in one piece. If it wasn't too late.

Someone shouted, 'Where's the captain?'

David turned. 'Right here. How many saws have we got? OK, Edward, take a man and check out the left side. Find out what the hell's really holding this tree up. We can't take a chance on its settling until we've got the car out.' He could see crumpled metal, just the back corner. What could the rest be like? He forced air into his lungs, called out, 'Get more lights up here! Pull the pumper around.'

Julie was almost positive she could smell petrol fumes. She had told herself it was her imagination, terror manufacturing the smell. She'd seen the light flaring—something yellow and brief, then sputtering again, not close, just dimly seen through the branches. The tree must have fallen through the electric lines, maybe brought down a pole. And——

So dark. The glass of the windscreen was all bumpy and dark and leaning towards her. Safety glass. Windscreens didn't splinter. If they had, she would have been a mass of cuts, probably bleeding to death.

The tree must be wet from the rain. Would it catch fire? Burn and take her with it? Everything would go up in flames when those fumes reached wherever the electricity was...

She was *not* going to cry. Stupid to cry. No one would hear. She could feel the pressure on her shoulder—the roof of the car. Her head was aching—injury or panic, she was not certain which. Although she tried, she could not remember the instant of impact.

David. She felt the tears then, because this could not happen to David again. To lose a woman he loved, to be alone and...if she had not been so stupid, trying to ask him for assurances. He loved her—he must! Maybe not enough, but—— What had she wanted? A rating? Julie scores five points above Sandy? Three points less? So stupid. If she had just held him close and taken what there was, instead of reaching for some thin air.

Coward, afraid to reach in case there was pain with the loving. There would be nothing now, just emptiness and loss. Her loss. His, because, whatever the damned ratings, he did care about her.

Light. Light from behind, slivers crawling through the branches. She tried to move, but couldn't. She could feel something prodding into her thigh from above. The steering column? Something from the front of the car, pushed back? The only thing she could move was her left hand, but the handle to roll down the side window seemed to be gone. That window was broken too, shattered but still in place. It probably wouldn't roll down anyway.

The lights must mean help, but it was too late. The fumes——

She should turn the engine off. Should—— No, it was quiet already. No sound, although—— Had she already turned it off? She couldn't remember that. Must have.

David. Why had she not gone after him when he walked out? Caught his arm and said, Don't go! Don't walk out on me! I need you ... love you.

Or listened to Molly. Don't run. Go back.

Running, David had said. Always running. So stupid ...

Voices in the dream—David's, shouting. No, that was wrong. Someone cutting down a tree ... Patrick, felling trees with a chain-saw to build his house. No, lumber from the ... David, coming with the bulldozer, pushing roots and soil away. Patrick and Tom building ... No, that was old stuff. David telling her Tom was too old for her. Too old. Too young.

David ... David, blanking out the moon. The smell of hay. Such a beautiful smell, fresh hay and love ... here any minute. David. No, no chain-saw. All that petrol. Fumes ... explosive. David. Explosive ... fight until she could close her eyes and his arms around her.

Safe. His baby would have dark hair. Suckling at her breast, sweet...

So lonely... without... without...

His face through the broken window. Terrible, monster tree. Belonged up with branches in the sky, not down here clinging to her, smothering her.

David...? He was calling her. Was he——? No. The fumes, or just losing it. No sense. Dreams, cool air, noise everywhere. Julie kept her eyes closed. Too bright. Dream light. His touch on her cheek, gentle rough. His voice... get you out of here.

'Stuck,' she muttered. 'Molly was right.'

The dream said something about hanging on and could she move. She whispered, 'I was afraid you wouldn't come.'

'I'll always come.'

So much easier in dreams. If she could remember the words, tell the dream. Always come... always dreams.

CHAPTER ELEVEN

JULIE turned on to her stomach, burying her face in the pillow, seeking warmth. The sounds intruded, gentle murmuring.

David's voice. Just David, no one else. The telephone?

That monster tree coming down out of no-where, smashing her car to nothing. Only a dream, a tangled dream, because it was David's dump truck that had really smashed——

She rolled on to her back, eyes closed, straining to listen. Footsteps. The wind... wind was gone. She opened her eyes. White ceiling, dresser. Not David's dresser with that picture smiling at him. Sandy. He'd been so angry, shouting at her, horrible things, hurting.

'Awake?'

David. He seemed giant, standing beside the bed, face harsh and older, hands hanging by his sides.

'Did a——?' She cleared her throat and tried again. 'Did a tree really——?'

'Yes. It's over now. You're safe.' He brushed her hair back tenderly. 'How do you feel?'

She closed her eyes, admitting, 'I dreamt you there, in the branches.'

He had undressed her, covered her with a thick, warm quilt. Now he bent down and touched her face, his finger brushing along her cheek. 'I've got some hot soup for you. Sarah sent it over.'

Stilted words. His. Hers. He was gone, then feeding her as if she were a child sick in bed.

'Where is this? Sarah's?'

He filled her lips with the spoon again. She was uncertain what happened next. Sleep? Then they were talking over her, David and the doctor. She knew it was a doctor, fingers on her wrist for her pulse. Voices, fading in and out.

'Better now... warm... a few hours... in tomorrow.'

'... hospital?'

'... not necessary. Just call me if she's not...'

*   *   *

She woke next with the sun on her face, blazing through a window, a brilliant day with no trace of rain or clouds. She sat up, felt the dizziness and got up anyway. Cool floor, not warm like David's.

Where was she?

There was a robe hanging on the end of the bed, an old four-poster bed. A big down quilt, the kind women had used to labour over for weeks and months. Julie remembered David's mother working on one like that, years back, a faint summer memory from the farm. She belted the robe and steadied herself as she went through the doorway into the next room.

She jumped at David's voice, flat and harsh.

'You shouldn't be up.'

There he was, surging to his feet from a big easy-chair, abruptly at her side, hands on her arms. 'Are you all right?'

'Yes.' She realised that she didn't sound all right. 'Where...?'

'The guest house.' His eyes swept down the length of the belted robe and his lips turned rigid with annoyance. 'And you've no business getting out of bed in bare feet.'

'What guest house? And I'm not——'

'Julie! For once in your life, *don't argue.*' He took her in his arms and she was swept up, swiftly laid on to a big, overstuffed sofa. 'Stay there!'

She closed her eyes, felt something heavy and warm settling over her a moment later. 'Feels like a dream,' she murmured. 'But you're shouting at me. Got to be real.'

He made an exasperated sound, then somehow she was tangled in his arms, the quilt and David imprisoning her with warmth. 'Go back to sleep,' he said tenderly. 'You're not yourself. I need you in your right mind before I can talk to you.'

'I'm there,' she insisted, burrowing deeper. 'What guest house?'

Was it laughter in his voice? 'Up the hill behind the farmhouse, in the trees. Mom and Dad built it years ago for their in-laws. They use it when they're here.'

'Why——?'

He sighed and pressed lips against her temple. 'Shush!'

'No. Why do you want me in my right mind?'

He almost smiled. She felt the lips moving against her cheek. 'So you can do a better job of arguing with me.' She struggled to sit, but his arms defeated her. 'And because I don't want to have to say it all twice.'

Her head thudded and she was very still. His arms were holding her very close. Surely if it were goodbye, he would not hold her like this? She whispered, 'Why did you bring me here? Why not——?'

'Because it's a neutral place.' He shifted until she settled back against the arm of the sofa, still in his arms, but she could see his face now. She struggled to free one hand from the quilt, reached her fingers and found his cheek rough with the growth of his beard.

'I need a shave,' he said, his voice oddly unsteady. 'With everything else——'

'Would you kiss me?' Incredibly, her voice was steady, but her eyes were wide and vulnerable, her lips parted and trembling.

He sighed, and his lips closed over hers, his arms drawing her closer as he softly explored the tremulous sweetness of her mouth. When he drew back, his eyes were black and filled with emotion.

'David...?'

He brushed her hair back with one hand, holding her close with his other arm. 'Julie, I——' His eyes closed and he said harshly, 'I thought I'd lost you.'

She ran her fingers down his cheek, found his lips and traced their firm fullness. He said abruptly, 'When you—— Yesterday, when you pulled away from me and told me——'

'Don't,' she whispered. She covered his lips with outspread fingers. 'I'm sorry. I should never have—— You don't have to say anything.' Sandy had given him fifteen years. If Julie was lucky, she would be able to count her time in years. Time for their love to grow strong.

David shook his head, imprisoning her fingers with his. 'Sandy was my wife, the mother of my child, the first woman I loved. She—we had a good marriage.'

Julie closed her eyes, knowing she had to accept this. He loved her too. He *did* love her, even if it would never be quite as much, quite as deep.

He said, 'I never wanted more than that. It was—easy, loving her. She fitted into my life, my world. And I didn't want my life turned upside down.'

Julie had been thirteen, sitting on the fence watching David do something with a cow in the paddock. She had hugged herself, stared at him, probably with her childish heart in her eyes, and asked, 'David? When I grow up, will you marry me and we can live in the farm-house and have children and be Mr and Mrs McNaughton?' She shook off the old image, and said quietly, 'I understand, David. You told me she was . . . perfect. You——'

'Damn it, Julie!' She could feel the tension through his chest, his arm behind her, his fingers in her hair. He closed his eyes and said raggedly, 'Can't you understand how damned difficult it was? A thirteen-year-old girl telling me she loved me? I wanted to hug you, to tell you how special you were, but that didn't change that it was impossible. Sandy and I— the baby on the way. I tried—I was trying to tell you about love, that you'd have that some day too.'

She slid her fingers along his cheek. It would be enough, somehow, whatever she could have. She could feel the restlessness in him. Then he sighed deeply and was still.

'It was true, Julie. Sandy was all I wanted. Someone who cared about the same things I did, a partner on the farm, peaceful. We never argued.'

She closed her eyes, whispered painfully, 'Do you have to tell me this?'

His hand caught her chin and forced her eyes up to meet his. She could see only dark pain as he said harshly, 'If I'd never come close to you as a woman—— Then, what Sandy and I had together might have been enough forever. We had—— It was good, Julie. We loved each other. But we could have been together for fifteen years, and I would never have known with her...what you've always stirred in me.'

Her breath was half tears. 'What? Anger? Disapproval?'

His eyes darkened. 'Every kind of emotion. I'm not a man of words, Julie. I can't——' He covered her lips with his and groaned, 'You always got inside the places I thought I could control, turned me—emotions deeper and wider and thicker... I don't know what the hell you want of me.' His eyes closed as he said in a jagged voice, 'If you walk out of my life, it will be like flatland to a man who's learned the feel of the mountains.' He stood up, freed himself of the quilt and her outstretched hand. He said raggedly, 'You can leave if that's what you have to do.'

She whispered, 'What if I stay?'

Some flash of humour lit his eyes. His lips turned down. 'You could try asking me to marry you again. It would be different this time. You're a woman now.'

She felt the breath short in her chest. It would be . . . better than dreams. Real life, his arms around her. Waking to his touch, looking out of the window and knowing he would come home to her. Always.

He said, 'Flames and fire and loving. Can you take the heat?'

'Are you daring me?'

Those dark eyes she loved bathed her in a warm smile. 'You always were a sucker for a dare.'

She swallowed. 'You said I was a coward.'

His voice turned dark. 'I always thought I was a practical man, but you drive me to—— I might have said anything.'

'I—I don't like cows, David.' Her heart was a hard, steady beat. 'Except on the other side of the fence.'

'I've got a hired man already,' he said soberly.

'I wouldn't mind collecting eggs some-times. I like the brown ones.'

'They're all brown. My chickens lay brown eggs.'

She felt the trembling that was growing from her centre. 'We'd fight. You know we'd fight.'

'Hm. Yes, but not as much as you think. Not now.'

'And...' she closed her eyes, whispered shakily '...and I'd want to have babies, and you've already done that and you won't want——'

David turned her hand in his, staring at her open palm as he said quietly, 'We'll get one of those packs and I'll take the baby with me when you're out teaching. There's a special education school in Nanaimo, and they've got to need someone like you. You could change, couldn't you? Another job——'

'David——'

'And we've got baby-sitters all over the neighbourhood. Molly and Pat, Sarah. Even Sally will soon be old enough to—— Stanley can learn to change nappies too, when he's home for holidays.' David closed his eyes and she felt his hand tighten on hers. 'The first time I made love to you, I hadn't meant it to happen that night, hadn't—— When I thought you might have my child, I found myself praying that you were pregnant, that I could tie you to me somehow. I knew it was the wrong way. It was the one thing that was always between Sandy and me, that she'd tried to trap me with the baby. But if I could have found a way to tie you to me—— I knew it was...but I needed you so desperately.'

'I love you,' Julie whispered.

'Oh, darling...I dreamed you would.' He crouched down beside the sofa, his fingers tangling in her curls. She saw his eyes deep and unshielded. 'Are you going to ask me to marry you again? Or do I have to do it myself?'

She asked shakily, 'Do you love me?'

'Always. So much.'

'I was so afraid that you couldn't. I...so will you marry me?'

He pulled her close.

She slid her arms around him. 'Does that mean yes?' The answer was in his eyes. Breathlessly, she entreated, 'Could you take me back to bed and just—hold me?'

She felt the quilt trailing as he carried her into the bedroom. He lowered her gently to the soft mattress and came down after her, tangling her in his arms and drawing her hips against him with one thigh thrown across her legs. 'Get used to it,' he said in a low voice. 'You're going to wake this way every morning for the rest of our lives.'

She closed her eyes and breathed in his scent. 'I'll give my notice, at the school. But I'll have to finish my contract.'

'The rest of the school year? Too long.' He kissed the tip of her nose. 'Have you room for me in that condo of yours?' He circled her shoulder with a lazy caress of his fingers. 'The Department of Agriculture's been after me to work on an experimental programme in Richmond, commuting distance to Vancouver. I told them this morning that I'd give them nine months.'

She burrowed closer. 'But aren't they closed? Sunday? You can't live in the city. You'd hate it!'

'Hush!' He took her mouth in a deep, shattering kiss, then said huskily, 'Yes, they are closed. Yes, it's Sunday, but I've got the director's home number. And I can't live *anywhere* without you.' He kissed his way from her mouth to her ear, teased the lobe with gentle teeth. 'In any case, if I give the farmhouse to the hired hand, I'll need time to get the new house built. I'm not about to wait nine months to marry you.' He laughed and said huskily, 'Nine months is long enough to do a lot of things. I wouldn't want to waste it.'

She felt something stir in the place where his child would grow. 'New house...?'

His eyes sobered. 'My darling, when you're in my arms, in my mind, my soul...there's no one but you in the world.'

Her eyes filled with moisture. 'David——'

'I thought we could build a new house, down in the hollow, that spot where the dogwood is. Our home.'

'You wouldn't cut that tree down?'

David traced the shape of her jaw, the vulnerable curve of her throat. 'We could have that tree outside our living-room window.'

'Oh!' she breathed. 'I've never seen it blossom. I—— It's too much, David. I don't need a new house.'

'We'll get an architect out, have some drawings done.'

'Just tell me again that you love me. That's all I need.'

'When you're away from me, it's a pain...emptiness.' He groaned against the softness of her shoulder, pressed his lips in a tender caress. 'Loving you, needing to know you're just a touch away. I want to build a dream home for us.'

'Your family? What will they...? That perfectly good farmhouse, and——'

'They'll say it's time David spent some money on something other than his damned cows.'

She could easily imagine Patrick saying that. She heard her own laughter, soft and joyous. 'But——'

'Stop arguing,' he said softly. He moved and somehow the quilt was gone. He murmured, 'I hope you're not still in shock.'

She gasped at his touch, stumbled over words. 'How can you leave the farm for so long? How——?'

'Hush,' he murmured against her throat. 'Trust me.'

She managed to ask softly, 'What if I don't stop arguing? I—I kind of like stirring you up. I—oh, David . . .'

He murmured softly and moved against her, telling her in the oldest way of a man and a woman that this was one battle they could both win.

MILLS & BOON NOW PUBLISH
EIGHT LARGE PRINT TITLES A MONTH.
THESE ARE THE EIGHT NEW TITLES
FOR MARCH 1992

———————— * ————————

WHEN LOVE RETURNS
by Vanessa Grant

DANGEROUS INFATUATION
by Stephanie Howard

A CURE FOR LOVE
by Penny Jordan

DEEP WATER
by Marjorie Lewty

ISTANBUL AFFAIR
by Joanna Mansell

ROARKE'S KINGDOM
by Sandra Marton

UNDERCOVER AFFAIR
by Lilian Peake

GHOST OF THE PAST
by Sally Wentworth

MILLS & BOON NOW PUBLISH
EIGHT LARGE PRINT TITLES A MONTH.
THESE ARE THE EIGHT NEW TITLES
FOR APRIL 1992

———————— * ————————

THE STONE PRINCESS
by Robyn Donald

SAFETY IN NUMBERS
by Sandra Field

LOVEABLE KATIE LOVEWELL
by Emma Goldrick

GOODBYE DELANEY
by Kay Gregory

THE TROUBLE WITH LOVE
by Jessica Hart

TWO-FACED WOMAN
by Roberta Leigh

DIAMOND FIRE
by Anne Mather

DEVON'S DESIRE
by Quinn Wilder